Frosting on the Cake 2: Second Helpings

by

Karin Kallmaker

Bella
BOOKS

2010

Bella Books, Inc.
P.O. Box 10543
Tallahassee, FL 32302

First Bella Books edition 2010

Editor: Katherine V. Forrest
Cover designer: Linda Callaghan

ISBN 13: 978-1-59493-205-2

"The Curve of Her" appeared in its original form in *Back to Basics: A Butch-Femme Reader*, 2004, Bella Books

"Filled to Overflowing," "Gladiators" and "Cruising Solo" appeared in their original form in *In Deep Waters 1: Cruising the Seas*, 2007, Bella Books

"Payout," "Twenty-One" and "Lucky 7" appeared in their original form in *In Deep Waters 2: Cruising the Strip*, 2008, Bold Strokes Books

About the Author

Karin Kallmaker's nearly thirty romances and fantasy-science fiction novels include the award-winning *The Kiss That Counted*, *Just Like That*, *Maybe Next Time* and *Sugar* along with the bestselling *Substitute for Love* and the perennial classic *Painted Moon*. Short stories have appeared in anthologies from publishers like Alyson, Bold Strokes, Circlet and Haworth, as well as novellas and short stories with Bella Books. She began her writing career with the venerable Naiad Press and continues with Bella.

She and her partner are the mothers of two and live in the San Francisco Bay Area. She is descended from Lady Godiva, a fact which she'll share with anyone who will listen. She likes her Internet fast, her iPod loud and her chocolate real.

All of Karin's work can now be found at Bella Books. Details and background about her novels, and her other pen name, Laura Adams, can be found at www.kallmaker.com.

Acknowledgments

Without readers, none of this would make any sense at all. Thank you for the support, the love and the willingness to let the journey take you wherever it goes.

In memory of Pam Butler, super fan, super woman.

Twenty-four and there will be more.

visit www.kallmaker.com

Table of Contents

To the Reader—

Revisiting my characters is a journey of love and I was delighted when I undertook this project. It also gave me a chance to gather eight short stories I'd written in the years since the first *Frosting on the Cake* collection and then write nine more. Some of the previously written stories were designed to fit a theme in an anthology, so these versions have additional material or changes so they stand on their own in this collection. *Happy New Year, Too* was originally released as a gift to readers, so this is its first time in print.

As with the first volume, the section at the end represents my notes about the manuscripts, answering many of the questions I routinely receive about where a character or plot came from.

The information given after each story's title tells roughly how much time has elapsed since the end of the novel. These stories are presented in the order that I felt would be the most enjoyable when reading the book cover to cover. You can decide if you want to read in that order or go directly to the story(ies) from your favorite novels. When it comes to cake there are no rules.

—Karin

Above Temptation

Published: 2010
Characters: Kip Barrett, private fraud investigator
               Tamara Sterling, owner Sterling Fraud
               Investigations
Setting: Seattle, Washington

Squee! O Glee! We are Twenty-Three!

Snap Judgment

(6 months)

"This is so cool!" Tam had to shout in Kip's ear. From their backstage vantage point, they had a prime view of the musicians. Tam was more than happy with her view of the AeroFlight drummer.

Drummers had amazing shoulders and PZDash, wearing skin-tight laser-blue leather vest and pants, was no exception.

Kip, standing on tiptoe, yelled in Tam's ear, "Roll your tongue back into your mouth!"

Tam spread her hands in a helpless gesture. What was she supposed to do? That was a fine specimen of lesbian musicality and wasn't it her sisterly duty to ogle? "The way you did at the Brandi Carlile concert last month?"

Grinning, Kip gave her a playful smack on the arm.

Her new job had certainly led them to new opportunities. Freelance financial fraud and security consulting for musicians was proving busy and lucrative, and Tamara Sterling was downright proud of her wife. Starting over wasn't easy, but Kip clearly loved the work. Kip was delighted to be *persona non grata* with several managers now and to bask in the undying love of a number of musical acts. AeroFlight would be her biggest to date, if they signed her to do an audit of their financial arrangements and advisors.

It wasn't all fun for Kip, though. While Tam had been watching the mesmerizing drummer—the whole show, really—Kip had been walking through the audience of the entire Pike's Dome, casually asking people for their ticket stubs. Some people wouldn't part with them, but with a clipboard and a copy of the latest *Rolling Stone* under one arm, her explanation that she was doing research for the band meant a number of people would give them to her, and answer a few questions.

"How do things look?" Tam asked. It was getting harder to be heard as the band entered the finale of their last set. The bass was painfully loud and she felt the vibrations through her shoes. Her heartbeat was trying to match the drums.

"Exactly what I thought."

"Really? That's so…retro."

"An oldie but a goodie. This can't be the first time this venue contractor has pulled this, and I of course have to wonder if someone is getting paid not to notice."

"If someone in band management is in on it that would explain why they're not playing Key Arena. Publicly owned—all those county auditors and annoying safeguards."

"I'm betting the whole band uses the same accountant and tax accountant for their personal finances."

Tam nodded. It was too loud now to answer. She felt so old, but she absolutely had to cover her ears—and she was to the side of the biggest amplifiers. She couldn't imagine being in front of them. The musicians wore ear jacks with noise reduction to spare their hearing, plus they got filtered playback of their own part of the performance.

Looking very smug, Kip fished in her suit pocket producing a set of ear plugs which she offered to Tam.

She mouthed "I love you" and was glad it was easy to lip read. Kip answered with a wink. Standing close together, they enjoyed the finale, the pyrotechnics, then two encores. At one point, Tam gestured at the towel behind the drummer, soaking up the perspiration running off the ends of her long, tight dreads. Before coming backstage with Kip at concerts Tam had not been all that aware of the demands of performances, but now she knew it was physically very draining. The bottles she'd figured were booze were actually full of Gatorade, and there were roadies charged solely with keeping them full. She thought that the number one reason some performers reached for drugs was exhaustion, plain and simple. AeroFlight was different in that they had their act together—a personal chef was backstage with a post-performance dinner that was as finely tuned as a pro athlete's training diet.

They'd have their act together even more if they hired Kipling Barrett. Since Kip had said so, Tam had no doubt that one of the oldest tricks in the book was costing each member of the band piles of money every time they went out on stage and literally sweated buckets for the crowd. She also had no doubt that Kip had a solid idea of who was getting the money instead.

Goodness, but she really loved the woman. She was suspicious, tenacious, ethical and determined to make sure no-good people got what they deserved. All that, plus Kip was a cute little fireball of energy and life. And all hers.

Standing backstage, Kip pushed her ear plugs deeper, eager for the show to be over. Maybe some day she'd be sanguine about landing clients and able to enjoy the shows. She didn't blame Tam for watching the drummer—she was riveting. All those broad shoulder muscles, the deep mahogany skin andthe light glinting off her sticks when she twirled them made for a gorgeous image. But Kip was focused on the assignment at hand and her stomach knots were a little too tight to completely yield to the music. She was really glad Tam was enjoying herself.

All the reviews of prior performances said the band never added another encore, so she was reasonably sure they were about done. She'd been asked to make her pitch while the band members cooled off. She was trying very hard to be more of a night owl, but it was tough locating her tiptop professionalism and razor-sharp presentation skills at eleven p.m., especially when her potential clients were strung out on adrenaline and would, in less than an hour from the last note, be comatose with fatigue. It could be a very short meeting.

She had her standard recommendations to help them be more confident that their affairs were being handled honestly. She also had proof they were being ripped off at this venue. If it was happening here, it had probably happened elsewhere. It helped her flagging energy that the sheer mediocrity of the skimming scheme made her mad. Really, she wouldn't be surprised to learn it had been lifted right out of an accounting 101 textbook from the chapter "Stupid Things that Auditors Will Catch So Don't Even Think About It."

The moment the last encore was over she pulled out the ear plugs. She hated the way they made her inner ears feel—kind of slimy. The band members, soaked to their skins, poured backstage, already talking shorthand to roadies and each other about tonight, tomorrow, dinner, how tired they were, all of it salted with basic and heartfelt adjectives that would put a sailor to shame.

Tam gave her a quick hug. "See you at home later. Wake me if you need to—I want to hear how it went." With a little purr she added, "Wake me anyway."

The tingle all down her spine was distracting but wonderful. "Okay. Be safe."

"You too."

She watched Tam walk away, feeling that very familiar appreciation of the way jeans hugged her backside. There was also a twist of immediate longing for Tam to come right back, right this instant, and be close to her again. She hoped the feeling never went away. It had been a risk to love Tam, to leave her challenging and beloved career on the chance of so much more, and every bit of the risk had been worth it.

Journalists and bloggers were crowding around with questions, fans who'd won contests were being introduced and she knew the chaos would swirl for a while longer. She moved out of the way, waiting patiently near the dressing room corridor where a burly, grim-faced security guard checked anybody who wanted to get by him. She was hoping to catch the eye of her contact, PZDash, a.k.a. Pam Zannuck, to make sure she didn't have any trouble getting to the dressing room area.

Assistants must have received some kind of signal from the band manager because the energy abruptly changed. The musicians moved decidedly toward their dressing rooms and everyone else was unceremoniously herded toward the exit, even though some were still calling out to the band members. One enthusiastic young woman kept yelling, "I love you JD! I love you JD!"

Okay, Kip thought. Not exactly the romantic overture she would call promising. John Duffy, the lead singer, didn't turn around—nor did she expect him to.

She was just about to get left behind, so she stepped

forward and firmly called out, "Ms. Zannuck!"

The drummer turned, gave her an "Oh yeah" nod of recognition. "Hang on guys—we have to do the accountant thing tonight." She waved at Kip as she gave Kip's name to the guard, who scribbled it on his papers.

"Is that tonight?" Kip couldn't see the speaker.

"Yes it's tonight. I reminded everyone before the show, remember?"

"That was two lifetimes ago," someone else said. "I can't think."

"I can come back—"

Zannuck waved her to silence. Over her shoulder she said, "It's now or eight o'clock tomorrow morning."

"Bitch." It was fondly said, but Kip still didn't know who was speaking.

"Come on," Zannuck said to Kip.

They were immediately stopped by the band's manager, Steven Selcer. Like most men in rock and roll, he was tall, handsome and self-assured in black jeans and a black band T-shirt. Older than the band members by at least fifteen years, if not more, his "discovery" of AeroFlight had cemented him as a star maker. "It sounds like John really doesn't want to."

"He never wants to, Stevie. But we have to. Kip is totally highly recommended and she's based here in Seattle."

Selcer gave Kip a wary look. He earned no points with her by taking just a moment too long—as if it were an effort—to look all the way down from his six-two or six-three to meet her five-two gaze. "I'm not convinced there's anything to be gained."

"Give me ten minutes to convince you. All of you," Kip added, nodding at Zannuck.

Zannuck slouched her way past Selcer, gesturing at Kip to follow. "Everybody is tired, but we're wired too. Now is as good a time as any."

Aware of Selcer following close behind, Kip stayed close to Zannuck. The farther they got from the stage, the less glamorous the surroundings. She was on their turf, and the rules of business meetings held in board rooms where introductions and résumés were shared, business cards handed round and a PowerPoint presentation whirred on a projector didn't apply here. These performers weren't just wealthy, they were living eccentric lives way outside of the 9-to-5. Their hours were late, and the barrage of manic worship from fans was endless, as was the long line of hands out for some piece of the action. Kip was just another hand out—she had to prove to them that her services were worth every penny.

"John, Richie, Cal," Zannuck said, pointing her introductions as they entered the green room. The three other musicians all gave a small but not exactly enthusiastic wave. "This is Kip Barrett, the woman I told you about. Bill and Cheryl recommended her."

Dinner smelled delicious, and Kip hoped her stomach didn't growl. A basic, functional kitchen had been set up in the rear of the room. A chef busily whisked something in a bowl while microwaves hummed and two pots bubbled on hot plates.

The rest of the room wasn't exactly shabby, but the two long sofas and half-dozen chairs were worn and sagging. A repaired section of jaundice-colored wall suggested someone had partied way too hard, and not that long ago. She was glad of the aromas from the cooking; these sorts of spaces had an old building funk.

"A pleasure everybody. It was a stunning show. Thank you so much for letting me experience it."

There was a sort of group nod. John Duffy, ripped jeans and soaked T plastered to his lean form, was almost prone on the closest sofa. Richie Merrick and Cal Fuentes, guitarists, looked exactly the way Kip looked after an all-nighter as they slouched in their respective chairs. Selcer took another of the chairs and Zannuck chose to lean over the back of the sofa Duffy was sprawled on.

"I know you're all tired, so I'll try to be brief."

Duffy lifted one eyebrow. It eloquently expressed, "Yeah, right. Everybody says that."

"I'm not an accountant. I'm a fraud specialist," Kip began. "I'm extremely suspicious. I see conspiracies, collusion and incompetence everywhere. I ask rude questions. I'm mistrustful of answers. I'm a hard ass—"

Merrick's laugh was skeptical. He had just completed a flicked-glance survey of her small, slender frame.

She gestured at herself. "Deceptive packaging, I agree, which is useful sometimes. I'm a short hard ass. But guaranteed I will let you all off the hook. Hire me, empower me to poke into your financial affairs and if someone complains, tell them it's out of your hands. Blame that totally competent but really bitchy specialist. So that's the top of the list—I'm on your side and nobody else's. I work for the four of you. Everybody else is possibly a lying, cheating, thieving rat bastard."

"Okay," Fuentes said, after a transparently impatient glance toward the kitchen and its awaiting delights. "You're a hard ass. What does this get us?"

"When's the last time you had an independent tax advisor review the band's and your individual tax returns for appropriateness, completeness and proactive tax planning?"

"Haven't a clue," Zannuck said. She shifted from leaning on her elbows to resting a hip on the back of the sofa. "When was it Stevie?"

Kip waved a hand as Selcer started to speak. "I don't need an answer. Not right now. But that's an example of the kind of questions I'll be asking of you and your manager and your tax advisor. They can tell me whatever they want, but I will examine everything for you. I will verify that you got what

10

you were told you got, that the services were correctly paid for, that the person who did the review was independent and reputable."

Selcer bristled. "That's really offensive. You have to trust people you work with. Otherwise this business stinks."

"Told you, I'm suspicious. And unfortunately, from what I've seen, this business stinks regardless. There's too much money flying around to blindly trust anyone. Money brings out the worst in people and what's more, it makes you suspicious. But because you don't want to look untrusting, you don't ask questions when you should and your suspicions can't be resolved, even if they're groundless. Every so often, you need someone like me to ask those questions. If all is well, everybody sleeps at night."

She paused, but no one said anything. "Then there's the tedious stuff. I can sit for hours tracing a transaction, verifying lists, picking apart reports for their sources. I know full well that the single most tedious thing on the money side of the business is reconciling the box office. I'll audit that it's being done properly because I know it falls to the very bottom of everyone's To Do list."

"We don't have to worry about those." Fuentes crossed his legs and stretched, muscles rippling all along his chest. She had wondered why all four of them had been in a *VH1* feature titled, "AeroFlight: No Time for Ladies." Their rocket-to-stardom careers hadn't left any of them time for serious dating, according to the article. But it wasn't because there weren't plenty of women looking for the honor. They all dripped that sexy, power rocker vibe. She'd given Tam a hard time for ogling PZDash, but she had the vibe just as much as the guys did.

Merrick added, "All the box office is paid to Selcer Productions, then transferred to AeroFlight Limited, and then we get our cut. So we get out of having our own accounting people, thank God."

It might be almost midnight, but they were all reasonably alert and engaged. And as casual as their poses might be, they weren't uninterested. Clearly, none of them realized that giving complete control of the accounting to someone else without a verification loop of some kind was an open door to theft. She understood that they didn't have time. She had to make them see and understand that they urgently needed someone like her making sure other people were doing their jobs.

She paused long enough for a server to circulate through offering lemonade and iced tea. Kip declined. The men all had tea. Zannuck had lemonade.

"I'm not a tax accountant, but I will vet one for you. I'll randomly audit box office so no one knows when the laser beam scrutiny will be there. I'll make sure the people you trust are trustworthy."

"This is going to piss people off. Some venues don't allow it, either." Selcer casually draped an arm over the back of his chair, pulling his black tee tight across his chest. "This is all over the top."

Kip said smoothly, her gaze moving from musician to musician, "It'll be up to you, a decision you all make and carry out. The foundation of your financial affairs' security is independent examinations. Someone with a suspicious mind who works only for you making random checks on systems you trust to other people. Someone who'll say 'If the venue won't agree to me showing up in the middle of the show to look at their books, don't perform there.'"

Their attention span was wavering. The chef had ceased his flurry of activity, obviously waiting to plate and serve.

"One last thing," she said as she pulled the substantial stack of ticket stubs out of her small zippered portfolio. "Hire me, and I'll find fascinating stories like this to tell you."

It was awkward to bend over the coffee table in front of the sofa, but Kip had no other choice. She set the stack on the table and carefully spread them out, like a magician fanning out multiple decks of cards.

Duffy, who had slid almost entirely onto his back, struggled upright on the sofa. "This is a story?"

"It's the sort of story I find fascinating. And you will too."

"Ticket stubs?"

She looked him in the eye. "You see ticket stubs. I see the story of financial transactions." She gestured at the long row of card-stock rectangles that were left over when the ticket taker tore off the main ticket. "These are arranged in the venue's seating order. On my left is the orchestra, dress circle, box seats. On the far right we're up in the nose bleed seats."

She waited for it, hoping someone bit. If no one did, they weren't going to hire her.

Fuentes had risen from his chair, a frown creasing between his eyebrows. "Why are some of the stubs white and some yellow?"

Bingo.

"I'm guessing the box office will say they had two different rolls of card stock, and used up one color before starting the next."

They were all frowning, but it was Duffy who proved he had been listening in math classes. "If that were the case, why are there more yellow tickets for the cheap seats and white ones for the high end ones?"

"That's a question I'd ask for you. If the colors meant nothing, they wouldn't be telling us a story."

"It's a story that doesn't make sense," Zannuck said. "I hated statistics, but isn't that like, well, improbable?"

"Yes." Kip was aware that the manager had gone very still. She wasn't surprised. Selcer was smart. He'd have spotted this right off and nixed it—if he wasn't the one to suggest it or

13

hadn't been happy to go along with someone in the venue's office.

"Wouldn't the cheap seats sell first?" Merrick looked a little out of his depth, but he was clearly intrigued as he got up to lean over Duffy's shoulder.

Duffy shook his head. "They don't, remember? The first tickets are always down front, then front of the upper circle, then the middle of the first floor."

"Like I said, the color is telling us a story. And so is this." She carefully slid the stubs back into the stack without messing up the order. Turning the stack over, she fanned it out again, making her black, blue and green Sharpie marks visible.

"Green means the person who gave me the stub didn't know the answer to my question. Black means the ticket was bought with a credit card. Blue means cash. The box office didn't accept checks."

"Son of a bitch." Zannuck snorted. "You have got to be kidding me."

Merrick was shaking his head. "So why are all the yellow stubs marked with blue? Well, most of them—some are green."

"None are black," Zannuck said, pointing. "The fucking yellow stubs are tickets bought with cash. The box office is tracking cash and credit sales separately."

"There may be a perfectly honest explanation," Kip said. "It would be my job to ask the hostile, awkward, rude questions."

"They're skimming cash on us," Zannuck spat. She grabbed several of the stubs, turning them back over. "Look, they have different codes completely from the white. It's just like the mom-and-pop food joints we all used to work at. One receipt book for cash, the other for credit cards. Remember those days?"

Fuentes nodded, "Sure. If I wanted to keep the job I recorded half my hours and they paid me the other half in cash. So instead of the IRS, *we're* the ones getting ripped off by cash we never knew existed. The box office pockets it—never even tells us those tickets were sold."

"If they are indeed underreporting sales to you, this would be a very simple way to do it. It's also a simple thing to spot. Now it's true that cash sales have overall dwindled for concerts," Kip said. "But it's still also true that the younger crowd, the ones who are buying the cheap nose bleed seats, don't have credit cards, and so they pay cash after standing in line all night. Again," Kip added, "I am a suspicious person. I think you are owed answers and reassurance."

"Stevie," Zannuck said, "what do you think is up?"

They don't have a clue, Kip thought. There really was no telling how long it had been going on, then.

Without deigning to look at the stubs, he answered, "I think there's a reasonable explanation for it. This is an old theater with old methods. I'll ask tomorrow."

Kip started to shake her head in warning, but Duffy forestalled her objection. "No, I think Kip is going to ask."

"Now, John, let's not jump to conclusions…"

Four pairs of eyes, in unison, shifted their gazes from the ticket stubs to their manager. Kip had seen that kind of bond before. They had been a band since they'd been seniors in high school, gigged together all the way through college, and hit the big time three years ago. They performed together with such frequency, and with such intimate passion and energy, that there was a tangible bond that resembled that of siblings. When Pam Zannuck had come out in the first year of super stardom a hate group had picketed their next show. The three guys had opened the show with a rap to the protesters where many two-and four-syllable words rhymed with *truckers*.

The foursome would bicker, tease, even fight, but woe to the person who tried to hurt any of them. Selcer was a fool if he didn't understand that. There was no divide and conquer, no making them feel like ingénues who didn't get the business.

Stevie Selcer might be unemployed soon, Kip thought. And Buck, her go-to guy for all things involving background checks and information ordinary mortals couldn't wring out of cyberspace, was going to be a busy fellow for the next couple of days. The money had gone somewhere. Somewhere maybe where she could even get at least some of it back.

There was a long, harsh silence while the musicians stared at their manager. Then Fuentes and Merrick returned to their previous chairs.

"Do you have a contract?" Duffy asked Kip.

"I do. I would want all four of you to sign it. I would work for all four of you. Your equal interests would be my concern. My arrangement is a retainer. I will use that for time and expenses. I hire highly trusted contractors for part of what I do, and I will pay them." She pulled a multipage document from her portfolio. "Copies for each of you. We would all sign each copy so everyone has an original."

Duffy turned to the last page. "Got a pen?"

Kip put her hand over the signature blocks. "Not now. Have some dinner. Talk it over. If you still want to sign, I'll be backstage to answer your questions. If you don't, just tell me, and I'll go on my merry way, no worries." She gestured at the ticket stubs. "You can keep those, regardless."

"Kip's right," Merrick said. "We need a band meeting before we decide about anything."

"Well, that means you all want to be alone," Selcer said with a congenial smile that didn't fool Kip at all. "I think this is all much ado about nothing, but you all decide what you want. I'm going to go make sure everything is battened down out there and the next security shift has arrived."

Moments later it was awkward that she and Selcer were on the same side of the green room door at the same time. She heard the hubbub of voices break out behind the closed door and moved purposefully toward the backstage area to avoid any appearance of eavesdropping.

"That was an impressive display." Selcer's expression was coolly bland. "I really think there's a simple explanation, and you'll be completely satisfied by their answers at the box office."

He thinks he can fix it before I get there, Kip thought. If he does then they might not hire me, but he's probably still fired. It wasn't an ideal outcome, but part of her would be satisfied. "It's an old scam, and an obvious one. Why didn't you see it?"

"I don't have to answer your questions. They haven't hired you yet." He didn't say "bitch" but she could practically hear him thinking it.

They weren't destined to be friends, so she asked, "I'm just wondering if it was laziness, incompetence or collusion that kept you from spotting it."

"Who do you think you are? You want a piece of it, fine."

"I want to put a stop to it."

He ignored her. "How much do you want? Ten percent?"

Kip paused deliberately, then said, "What would that amount to?"

He smiled at how easily she appeared to be capitulating. "Six figures. One time offer."

So casual, so practiced about it..."Before I came here I did my homework. I already suspected there was something to find. I even thought we might be having this conversation."

"And?" He glanced at his watch.

"You didn't do your homework, did you? You really don't know who I am."

"You're an accountant. You—"

"You *have* heard of Sterling Fraud Investigations, haven't you? The people who nailed Joseph Wyndham and his band of embezzlers? And those nasty stock portfolio derivative frauds from last year? Until a little over a year ago I worked for Sterling."

The very slightest hint of concern crept into his still smug expression.

"Now I'm married to Tamara Sterling. Do you think I have any interest whatsoever in your hundred thousand dollar bribe?"

There was a gasp and Kip turned to see Zannuck standing in green room's open doorway.

"Fuck you, Stevie!" She put her hands on her hips and fire seemed to lance out of her eyes. "Your ass is fired."

Kip couldn't have said it better herself.

Tam felt as if she was floating out of a good dream. Whoever invented beds should be canonized. Surely it had been a woman because sheets and warmth and pillows were divine. The new bedroom set she and Kip had acquired on their anniversary had proven a luxurious, decadent investment that encouraged oversleeping…and other pleasurable pastimes.

The shower was what had probably woken her. She rolled over to find Kip's side of the bed undented. Dawn was peeking around the drapes. She'd just gotten in?

The shower turned off and after a minute the light coming from under the bathroom door winked out. Soft footsteps crossed the carpet and then the covers on the other side of the bed rustled and the bed shifted slightly.

With a little murmur she feigned sleep as she flopped over onto the deliciously nude Kip.

"I woke you, didn't I? I tried not to."

She laughed. "It's okay—you were up all night?" Tam propped herself up on one elbow to peer at Kip in the dim light.

"It was a bloodbath. Sometimes things work out beautifully.

18

The manager offered me a bribe and a band member overheard him do it. So I spent the rest of the night doing the box office on the spot with the sexy, famous John Duffy watching. Pam and Cal made sure Stevie left the premises and the roadies and security knew where their paychecks were really coming from. Richie crashed so he could be up at six to call their attorney and see about freezing assets held in common before Selcer cleans the accounts out. Hey, I recommended Luke as a temporary manager for the rest of their stay here in Seattle while they try to secure a new one with the experience they need. They need someone on point and Luke can bring in some buddies he trusts."

"Jen will go on being your best friend because that's a nice bonus with their second baby on the way."

"I owe him. He got me my first lead."

Tam smoothed Kip's still damp hair, loving the silky feel against her fingers. "So did you get to spend any time with Pam?"

"Not really." Kip smiled up at her. "Yes, she's gorgeous. But darling, she's not my type."

Trying to hide a smile, Tam pretended to be hurt. "Gorgeous isn't your type? What does that make me?"

"Any woman who isn't you isn't my type. And that makes you mine." She arched up to feather kisses along Tam's jaw. At the same time, one hand found Tam's breast. "I love it when you're all soft and melted and sleepy."

"Not so sleepy now," Tam whispered. Her body felt as if it had just burst into flames. A light brush of fingertips along her hip drew a moan deep from her throat. In a sudden fever, she found Kip's mouth and shared a kiss full of impatient intentions.

She loved Kip's hands. They were small but strong and very sensitive. Her experience was limited, but she had never been touched by anyone with such precise care and such attention to shades of sensation, who watched her face for every responsive nuance. In what seemed like only heartbeats she was straddled over Kip, her face in the pillow above Kip's shoulder, panting desperately while Kip's fingers found and woke up every last nerve between her legs.

"I love you," Kip whispered. "And being inside you when you're like this is incredible. *Please*."

The plea touched her in places only Kip's voice ever reached. She gasped, then rocked back with a plea of her own.

It took a minute for her to realize that, as she had drifted in a very pleasant frame of mind, Kip had fallen asleep.

She was pretty sure the sun was up now, and she studied Kip's profile, wanting to kiss the lips that were lightly curved in a relaxed smile. Her love needed some rest though. It occurred to her that if she got up now, she could get a great deal of work done while Kip slept, and that would give them Sunday afternoon together.

Congratulating herself on a fantastic plan, she carefully slithered out her side of the bed. Her knees felt deliciously weak. She took one more long look at Kip and decided that she had even more fantastic plans for the afternoon. And the evening. She had so many fantastic plans it would take a lifetime to try them all.

The Kiss that Counted

Published: 2008
Characters: CJ Roche, commercial realtor
               Karita Hanssen, legal receptionist, battered
               women and children's shelter volunteer,
               animal shelter volunteer
Setting: Denver, Colorado

Twenty. Who knew? Little perennials,
where did they come from?

It's...Complicated

(2 years)

"And one last signature here, I promise." CJ pointed to the final dotted line, confident that her pounding heart was audible only to herself.

J. Anthony Gates, captain of Denver industry, knew that it took time to sign a contract like this one, and hadn't shown any impatience. Their waiter was also experienced enough to have ceased hovering and left them alone while the papers were on the table. Even though nobody was ordering two-hundred dollar business lunches these days, they'd ordered enough—and CJ was a frequent enough visitor—that the waitstaff had no worries of it being worth their while to let them linger long after their last morsel was consumed.

She felt her iPhone vibrate in her pocket again—fifth time

in twenty minutes. It couldn't be Karita. She knew today was the big day and that CJ was coming home with the fattest commission check of her already successful career. Their partnership worked out in the best way possible when it came to finances. CJ did the one thing she was so good at, making people give up their money, and Karita did the many things she was so good at, like nurturing frightened animals, women and children at the two shelters where she volunteered. When her sweetie wasn't doing that she was taking the second of her teaching certification courses in the long-term goal of teaching Vietnamese to immigrant kids. That her blonde Norwegian-extract girlfriend spoke fluent Vietnamese was just one of the many facets of Karita that made her a rare and wonderful jewel.

Love has made me mushy, CJ thought. She watched J. Anthony Gates pen his last signature and raised her wine glass. "Cheers!"

He joined her in another sip. "That's a huge relief."

"I've never seen deals like this in the past ten years, and your research and development campus is going to be at rock-bottom cost for the next ten for you."

"You made it happen. How come you don't work for me?"

CJ laughed. "I like what I do."

His fifty-something face creased into a smile. "Hard to argue with that. Oh, plus there's this."

He handed her an envelope. Eyebrows arched, she opened it and extracted a check.

She gasped, and pressed a hand to her heart. "Tony—that's wonderful. Thank you! You have no idea how far this money will go and how many women and kids are going to be helped."

"Actually, I do. My own sister married a creep and I only found out last month she has been in a shelter repeatedly over the last five years. She was too embarrassed to tell anyone."

CJ tucked the check for twenty-five thousand dollars

back in the envelope. Emily, the director of the women's shelter she frequently wrote fundraising appeals for, would be overjoyed. The brutal economy had both dried up donations and increased the need for beds as frustrated people—mostly men—took out their anger on their families. "It's sad, but I think most people don't know that they know someone who is getting beat up at home."

"I remembered that before we even started talking about this deal you had been a signer on a fundraising letter I got. I round filed it—I give lots to the alma mater and Jerry's Kids. Still, I can't beat the crap out of her husband, but I can do this."

"And get her a good divorce lawyer." Not that anyone in the entire Gates family couldn't afford the best.

He sighed. "She's not ready for that. I just don't get it."

Because you've never thought love actually had that kind of price, CJ wanted to say. She knew more about that than she would ever tell anyone. Karita knew some of it, that was enough. All her debts to anyone were paid, and she was done with the past. There was just the future.

Her phone vibrated again. It couldn't be her office, either; they knew what she was doing. Burnett was no doubt hunched over his desk, waiting for a text before he celebrated. As her associate, he was getting a large chunk of the action too. Well, whoever it was would have to wait.

They both passed on dessert, but when the waiter suggested a fresh fruit and cheese plate it sounded so healthy, they decided to split it. Right, CJ thought, cheese is healthy after a full lunch. She couldn't resist the richly veined blue or the soft double cream brie.

When she finally left the dark confines of the restaurant the bright spring sun felt wonderful. The sky was the kind of blue that made her realize that most other blue skies she'd ever seen really weren't. She had a multi-million dollar contract tucked in her satchel and a commission guarantee that paid out for ten years. It was a *beautiful* day. The client's thanks were still ringing in her ears when she finally checked her phone display.

The last message was from Nann, the director of the animal shelter where Karita volunteered. It said, "Everything's fine."

Shit. That was never good.

She scrolled back through the messages as she got into her Trailblazer. All from Nann. Reading backward, the half-dozen missives said that everything was fine, could she get in touch soon, don't worry, you should probably come on up, the paramedics say she's okay, and the very first message said "I think she's okay, but they're checking her out now." There was no question in CJ's mind as to who was being checked out. It had to be Karita. It would *of course* be Karita.

There were no other messages. What was it this time? Had she fallen off a roof trying to rescue a kitten? Been bitten by a llama trying to avoid their notorious spit? Sprained an ankle chasing a stray? This had better not be an April Fool's joke!

She tried not to panic as she backed out of the parking space. That there were no messages from Karita was unusual. Most of the time, when Karita had a misadventure, the first message read, "So sorry, I'm okay. Update when you get home. It's complicated."

Once safely on the street—she was not risking attention from the Denver traffic cops ever again—she called Karita. No answer. Then she tried Nann. No answer.

Even distracted, it was always easy to head home. All she had to do was point the nose of the car toward the mountains. The hard part was surviving the traffic. It didn't help that it was a Friday afternoon and a late season blizzard had brought good skiing as close as Loveland. Highway 74, the quickest route to their home near Kittredge, was clogged with four-wheel drives trying to go 90 in a 55 when 30 miles per hour was the best anyone would do. Skis and snowboards strapped on top made it difficult to see beyond them. Adding to the stop-and-go was a concert at Red Rocks and the races at Bandimere Speedway.

She tried Karita, she tried Nann—damn, she was close to the Hogback and the reception was breaking up. The signal at the animal shelter was never much good, but her own location was compounding the matter.

Traffic picked up a little once she got past Red Rocks. The bar count on her phone bounced up and down like a heart monitor, then went to zero and stayed there. No more texts, nothing. Neither of them were answering.

Finally, just passing Idledale, she got a strong signal and Nann's phone rang instead of going directly to voicemail.

"What's up?"

"Don't worry, CJ. She's going to be fine. They put a liter of—" The connection crackled furiously. CJ wasn't sure, but she could have sworn that Nann said the word "bear" before the call dropped.

Don't worry? *Don't worry!?* She resisted the urge to lean on her horn, not that it would do any good on a two-lane highway. She'd be there in three minutes.

She lived a lifetime in three minutes. She could imagine the darkest things, fed by her own memories of childhood. She knew what blood smelled like, had seen beatings that were probably nowhere near the damage a mauling by a bear would do. Karita could be so foolish, so blissfully unaware of danger, and unable to believe that bad things happened. CJ had seen her stand in front of a maniac with a baseball bat, saying "No," like that would work. She had nearly gotten her skull bashed in.

The turnoff to the animal shelter was still a minute ahead when her eye was caught by flashing lights deep in the pines and firs along a dirt road. There was a flash of yellow that might have been Nann's car, so she quickly swerved and turned. Her Trailblazer had no problem with the deep ruts and steep climb from the low bridge that spanned Bear Creek. Her hands were trembling on the steering wheel.

It was Nann's car all right. There was also a fire engine and an ambulance, red and blue lights still circling and flashing.

She was coasting to a stop when she saw Karita's car.

What was left of Karita's car.

The passenger door to the old Subaru had been ripped out of its moorings, and it hung by one bolt on the lower hinge. Stuffing from the seats was shredded and the passenger seat was halfway out of the gaping door. Scratches along the damaged frame were deep and long and the roof and hood looked as if something large had danced on them.

There was no sign of Karita.

CJ couldn't breathe. *Nann said she was okay*. She had to trust it, even as she whispered, "God, please no."

Getting out of her car wasn't easy. She felt so strange—part of her ran screaming across the clearing, frantic to find Karita. But the rest of her could hardly move.

"CJ!"

She turned her head too quickly and thought that if she fainted there was at least an ambulance handy.

Nann was waving at her. "This cell phone is worthless, I swear."

Like that mattered. "Where is she?"

"In the ambulance. She's got the attendants laughing of course."

"Laughing." Sure enough, the sound of a man's throaty guffaw reached her ears. "Laughing. Nann, for heaven's sake, what happened to the car? What happened to her?"

"She'll have to tell you what happened. It's—"

"I know—I know! It's complicated. It's *always* complicated!"

Nann gave her the indulgent look she saved for overwrought people and animals. "Given the circumstances, she did pretty well."

Shaking with reaction and anxiety, CJ crossed the pine needle-covered clearing, stepping over fallen branches and avoiding crusted ruts left in the dirt by run-off. It was a marvel that the Subaru had made it this far from the road. Between age and its light frame, it didn't have much oomph or traction.

She rounded the fire engine and saw two firefighters leaning against the open back doors of the ambulance. Both looked like they were having a coffee break around the station house cooler. The ambulance driver was having a smoke not far away.

The woman looked up at her with an almost annoyed expression, as if she was enjoying herself and had a feeling that CJ was a party pooper. "I think your girlfriend is here."

"CJ?"

Karita's voice, at last. Flooded with relief, she blinked back tears.

"Honey, what on earth did you do?"

"She's had a nasty scare, that's for sure," the male firefighter said. He was older and had that paternal air that Karita aroused in the men who didn't immediately want to date her.

Finally, she could see inside the ambulance.

Propped up on a stretcher, Karita smiled at her.

It might have made the world go right, it might have eased the trembling in CJ's stomach, but the sight of the amazing blue eyes nearly swollen shut and the long silver-gold hair matted with something oily knocked the breath out of her again. It was a few moments before her gaze traveled down to the large padding on Karita's left calf, which was elevated. The dressing was clean, but there was blood on the stretcher. A lot of blood, and it abruptly swam in her vision.

"Sit down," someone said in her ear, firmly prodding her.

She sat.

"Honey, I'm so sorry," she heard Karita say. "I don't know what I was thinking."

That bad things don't happen, CJ tried to say but her mouth wouldn't move.

"A bear cub ran across the highway, right in front of me. I nearly ran it over."

There was a long pause, and CJ finally felt clearheaded enough to focus on Karita's face. "And then what happened?"

"I followed it up here. I didn't actually get hurt until I tried to climb down out of the tree."

Okay, she was in the tree. "Why were you in the tree?"

"It was the closest thing after I got out of the car."

Okay, she had gotten out of the car to climb the tree. "Why did you get out of the car?"

"Well, I didn't think staying in the car made a lot of sense with a bear getting in there with me." Karita had that tone of something being patently obvious to her, and anyone who wasn't following along was a bit slow. "Do you think it can be fixed?"

"I can't even begin to think about that right now."

"I love that car—I'd heard bears could open car doors like sardine cans, but that was really something to see up close."

Just another interesting life-threatening event in the life of Karita Hanssen. "Honey, I don't care about the car. I really care about how you ended up in a car with a bear."

"I was never in the car with the bear. By the time the bear was in, I was in the tree."

CJ gritted her teeth. "Why was the bear trying to get in your car?"

"It wasn't so much in as through."

"Through your car. Why?"

"See, that's the part that's totally bizarre."

CJ laughed against her will. "Right. Up till now it's just an

30

everyday thing, you in the tree, your leg cut up and face like a balloon."

"Is it that bad?" Karita touched her fingers to her cheek. "It feels like it's going to pop."

The paramedic, who had been busy writing on a clipboard, chimed in with, "I have to admit, this is a first for me."

"Me too," Karita said.

"Me too," CJ snapped. "So—the bear?"

"The mama bear just wanted her cub."

"Oh my God, Karita, tell me you didn't put the cub in your car."

"Of course not!" What little of Karita's eyes that were visible blazed with indignation. "I'm not stupid."

My poor love, CJ thought. It all looked so painful and she wanted to hold her close except the paramedic was in the way and she couldn't make her arms obey her anyway and she *still* didn't know what had happened. "So why was the mama bear attacking your car?"

"I didn't mean to stop between them. The cub was running back toward me and I thought it was lost, so I stopped, but it wasn't running toward me, it was running toward its mom and I didn't see the mother until she hit the car with her shoulder—wow, I thought I'd go right over too. So the cub must have been just the other side of me."

"And the mama bear thought her baby was in the car."

"Or under it."

"So you got out of the car."

"You bet I did! That door just peeled right off, so I went out through the window, actually, and got on the roof."

CJ touched the bandage on her calf. "Did you get clawed?"

"Oh no. I got up in the tree, just fine. I had to go way up, though, because bears are smart. Mama stood up on the car and tried to follow me up the tree."

"So that's how the roof got dented."

31

"Yeah. Do you really think it's totaled?"

"Honey, I'm more concerned about you, right now. I'm glad *you* aren't totaled, you know?"

The firefighters chuckled. Great, they were getting the whole free family show.

CJ became aware that Nann had joined them. "I have to get back—glad you're okay, Karita. Don't come in tomorrow. I'll send you home if you do. Pam is going to drop in after work to help me out."

"It's only a little blood," Karita protested to Nann's departing back.

"Karita," CJ said explosively, "it looks like a *lot* of blood to me!"

"Not really. Well, not all at once. It wouldn't have happened except I couldn't see where I was going."

"Honey, I'm just trying to understand. You got up in the tree, but what did you do to your face?"

"I didn't do anything—but I didn't account for the wind, and then I got some pine pollen in my eye and forgot and wiped it. That's when it got bad."

"Sure, a bear ripping the car door off wasn't bad." CJ took a deep breath. Sarcasm was one of her strengths, but it wasn't a particularly helpful skill in getting information out of Karita. "Pine pollen did that to your face? Since when have you been that allergic to pine pollen?"

"Not the pine pollen, the pepper spray."

CJ rested her head in her hands. "Of course, what was I thinking? The pepper spray did it."

"I wasn't going to leave my purse in the car with the bear, it had my cell phone."

"And bears are well-known for identity theft," the paramedic said with a grin, but it turned to a gulp when he took in CJ's expression.

"A bear nearly killed you. I'd appreciate it if someone took this seriously." She nearly said, "It's not funny" which was guaranteed to make everyone else think it even funnier.

"Oh, we do," the female firefighter said helpfully. "There'll be a bill for the extension ladder."

"Pepper spray," CJ said wearily. Karita might have been killed, she thought, and everyone had to be a comedian.

"The mama bear was trying to climb the tree after me. So I got out my pepper spray." She spoke to the paramedic. "My boss at the women's shelter makes us all carry it now, for when we leave the shelter late at night."

"I got a twenty-five thousand dollar donation today for the shelter," CJ said. Oh *great*. Now I'm acting like nothing incredibly bizarre just happened, no, it's just business as usual. A bear tore off the car door. I got a big check today too, honey. Pass the sugar.

"Really? That's wonderful news!" Karita actually looked around as if she would find her cell phone. "We should call Emily."

"I think right now, if you called Emily, she would want to know how the hell you got covered in your own pepper spray. Maybe?"

Karita pouted slightly. "I told you. The wind."

"It blew back in your face?"

"No, that was lucky, it just got on my clothes."

Perhaps CJ's face did a better job of conveying her urgent desire for information, because Karita rapidly continued, "And I was careful, honest. I realized it could get into my face, so I knew I couldn't spray directly. I got a pine cone and sprayed that, then dropped it down toward the bear. It worked—one whiff and she took off, baby following her."

Finally, CJ had enough of the dots. "But you got something in your eye, and wiped your face with your hands…"

"Yeah. It's way better now, though."

Just since they'd been talking some of the raw swelling had

subsided, but it was still hard to imagine what it must have been like at first.

"We rinsed her with eye-safe saline and applied burn ointment. This is a pretty nasty case."

Finally, Karita looked sheepish. "I realized what I'd done with my hand and it was instinctive. I tried to wipe it off with my shirt."

"And your shirt was already covered with it. Oh, honey."

Karita gave a little sigh, suddenly looking hurt and tired. "My cell phone kept chirping that annoying signal dropped sound. I couldn't see. At least the bear was gone."

"So you tried to climb down?"

"Yeah, and scraped my leg on a branch. I sort of slipped. I could tell it was bleeding, but I didn't want to touch it with pepper spray on my hands."

It was starting to make sense, in a very Karita sort of way. As upset as she was with Karita's reckless decision to get involved in anything to do with bears, she now only wanted to take Karita home, tuck her in bed and hold on tight for the next year or two. "So how did you get down?"

"I kept trying to send out a text. I knew the last person I'd texted was Nann, so I was hoping I pushed the right buttons in the right order. Texts get through sometimes when there's not enough signal for a call. I thought I was typing *help*, but turns out I was typing G-W-K-O. She got four of those, then used the GPS locator."

She owed Nann a month of Sundays cleaning cages or something. Her imagination took off like a rat in a maze, circling around and around the pain and fear her sweetheart must have felt, none of which showed now. "Oh, honey…"

"I just want to go home, okay?"

"Can you?"

The paramedic nodded. "She's gotta sign here, and needs to have the stitches checked and be watchful for infection.

The tear was ragged—that's why it bled so much. No major arteries hit."

Karita sat up to sign the paper. "I'm really thankful you came so quickly," she told the paramedic.

"At first it came in as a bear mauling."

"I don't think I was making much sense when my friend Nann found me."

CJ snorted.

Working together, and with the woman firefighter lending a shoulder, Karita was able to hobble to CJ's car. Her face had further healed by the time she was buckled safely in place. CJ led the departing parade, followed by the ambulance with the fire engine bringing up the rear.

They had pulled into their garage when Karita said in a tiny voice, "Am I in trouble?"

CJ turned off the engine. She tried to be calm, but blurted out, "You scared me to death!" Then she burst into tears. "No, don't you dare try to take care of me—I'm just upset. You stay over there until I can help."

"I really don't know how it got so bad so fast."

"You *never* know," CJ said, still sniffling.

"That sounds like you don't like me much."

"Sweetie…" She started to lean across the car to give her a smooch, but Karita waved her away.

"Not a good idea. What if there's still some residual spray?"

"It was a bear, honey. Not a dog. Not a cat. Not even a llama."

"I thought it was lost."

"Not everything that wanders is lost."

"I know. I just…I know you think I'm a flake sometimes."

CJ took a deep breath. "You're not a flake. You have too much savvy about a lot of things that elude me to be a flake. I wish I saw the world the way you do."

"I promise not to ever follow a wild animal again."

"Good." CJ finally got out of the car. Without Karita's Subaru, there was plenty of space in the garage to maneuver. "Let's get you inside."

"Wait," she said. "I can't go in with these clothes on. The dogs will probably pick up the spray—so will the cats."

CJ laughed. She helped Karita get out of the car and did the only thing that made sense.

"Hey—at least close the garage door before you strip me."

CJ hurriedly triggered the door and once it was fully down went back to one of her favorite pastimes. "I never thought about having you naked in the garage."

"Well, it's not exactly a turn on right now."

For the first time, Karita sounded like she was in pain.

She pulled her close, lingering remnants of pepper spray be damned. "You know that I love you, don't you?"

"Yes, and I love you back. You put up with—"

"Shh. I'm getting you naked." Once she had bared one of Karita's shoulders, she planted a fervent smooch on it.

"Some day we'll think this is a great story." It came out as a question.

"Yes we will." CJ sighed. "Darling, life with you is complicated and never dull—but I could use a little less excitement."

Naked, Karita snuggled into her arms, averting her face from contact with CJ's clothes. "Shower?"

"Yes."

"Together?"

"Yes." She directed their steps toward the door to the house where the canine and feline audience awaited. "And then we'll go get soup in the village and talk about what you need in a car."

"Ice cream after?" Karita sniffed. "I feel like such a fool."

Wisely, Cocoa and Golden backed off, though their curly haired doodle tails wagged madly. The cats took one whiff and departed. CJ sent Karita toward the shower while she fished out two dog biscuits which sent the dogs to their respective gnawing places.

She had just reached the back of the house when she heard Karita urgently call, "CJ!"

Dropping her satchel, she hurried to the bathroom. She heard the shower running. "What is it? What do you need?"

Her voice floated over the top of the shower enclosure. "I just remembered—did you get the big deal?"

Relieved, she smiled. "Yes, I did."

Karita popped open the door and stuck her head out. "Congratulations," she said with a grin. Her hands were busy fashioning a Mohawk with the shampoo suds.

The sight of her love's still puffy and ruddy face below a white crown of foamy hair hit CJ's funny bone. Laughing, she stripped off her clothes and grabbed the shower massage gel. No matter what the adventure, one thing was certain— her love for Karita was never complicated. It was as simple as magic.

Warming Trend

Published:	2009
Characters:	Anidyr Bycall, doctoral candidate (glaciers) and bartender
	Eve Cambra, restaurateur
	Tan Salek, college administrator
	Lisa Garettson, cocktail waitress
Setting:	Key West, Florida
	Fairbanks, Alaska

Twenty-one! Finally of age, finally legal.

Good Morning

(1 year)

"Are you saying I shouldn't be wearing white?"

Lisa, big surprise, wasn't smiling when she turned away from the mirror.

Ani quailed. "No, that's not what I meant—I mean, I meant it, but not what you think."

"Like you're the Virgin Mary. Oh, I forgot, you *are*. You did that whole fell-in-love-for-the-first-time-and-turn's-out-she's-the-one thing. If you don't count the three years you didn't speak to each other."

Lisa's hands were on her hips. That was never a good sign.

"I only meant that you're so fair I'm not sure white looks right on you. Honest." Ani did her best big, dark puppy eyes. It worked on Eve. Well, sometimes.

"I don't know why I brought you with me."

"Because Eve and Tan are out shopping for Tan's tux, and I know less about that than I do about dresses. You're going to be a beautiful bride. It almost doesn't matter what dress you get."

Her hopes of having finally worded a compliment correctly were dashed with Lisa's toss of her thick, lush, sexy blonde hair.

"So that's what I'll tell my future wife? That I got just any old thing while she's out there looking at tuxedos?"

Ani put up her hands in defeat. "I give up. I can't please you."

That earned her a smile. "You don't really try."

"But I do try." She thought better of adding, "Tan is a saint for trying, and a god for succeeding."

Lisa went back to gazing in the mirror. "You really don't like this one, do you?"

Ani gave the dress another look. It was covered in big lace flowers, which Ani really didn't care for, but she didn't want her preference for simpler attire to get in the way of Lisa choosing a dress that suited her. The shaped bodice did show off Lisa's considerable assets, and it was fitted to make it look as if she had a waist the size of a toothpick. The skirt was cut asymmetrically, and maybe that was the problem. Lisa was very graceful, yet she looked lopsided.

Glad she didn't have to waste an "It makes your ass look fat" excuse, she finally said, "The skirt is lumpy, and you don't look like your usual lithe self."

Lisa frowned into the mirror. "It's hard picking a wedding dress on limited funds. This is what I get for coming to a department store."

"You weren't going to do this until summer, but we're here and health insurance awaits you if you do it now. It's a no-brainer. You put your money into the cottage—it's so beautiful.

And we're so glad to be able to share it with you. To be your first house guests."

"It was *such* a relief when Tan got that job."

"You both got lucky."

"But what were we thinking? Just because you guys were visiting we could throw together a last-minute for-real wedding? We should have made it a denim event, picnicked on the inter-island ferry and called it a day."

Lisa began shimmying out of the dress. Ani stood ready to assist. She was getting better about sparing Lisa's hair as the dress went over her head. Muffled by lace, Lisa continued, "Nobody is getting work in universities right now, and I can't say I was really happy to move to Massachusetts, but there was no turning it down. I'll be full-time at the Blue Harbor in a matter of months. I'm already pulling the highest shift tips."

Ani didn't doubt that. Behind that bombshell exterior and five-million-dollar smile was a ruthless adding machine born from too many exes walking away with too much of her money. Ani hadn't thought there was much of a heart until butterfly Lisa and the serious, reliable Tan had locked gazes for the first time. Ani hadn't known Tan had a sense of humor, but Lisa had found it within sixty seconds of their first meeting. Tan had brought out the steel-trap mind and made Lisa feel as if it was her sexiest trait among a bounty of sexy, appealing traits. Flattery sounded natural coming from Tan.

Ani supposed she herself always sounded a little grudging— and who could blame her? She wasn't put on this earth to regularly oil and lube Lisa's ego.

She tried to mollify Lisa with, "The falls are supposed to be gorgeous." She tugged slightly and Lisa was abruptly free of the gown. Goodness, the girl had assets. Ani's appreciation was purely academic, the same as she'd appreciate a painting. Her favorite assets were Eve's because they were, well, attached to Eve. She loved waking and finding Eve among the sheets and exploring how her assets were feeling any given morning. For half the year at home, Alaskan mornings looked just like Alaskan nights and some things were really better when well rested.

"But we can get married here, and our best friends are here, so let's have a wedding."

"Well, why not?" Ani did her best to position the dress on the hanger again. "Fairbanks will melt before it's legal in Alaska. Especially if voters get to decide what civil rights The Gays can have this week."

"In time," Lisa said. "Or you and Eve can move." She laughed at Ani's expression. "What am I thinking? You both actually like it there."

"Yes we do. We like it there." Ani smiled. She loved Eve's house—their house—and her nearly finished PhD and her research assistant teaching duties, and Eve's cooking and their dog Tonk and the puppy Tigr. Tigr was a recent addition, and they were all much tried by the relentless gnawing a husky puppy did. Eve had already lost two bras and Ani was out of old snow boots.

"Let's try that bridal shop in Natick," Lisa announced. "The prices are supposed to be bearable."

By the end of the day Ani's nerves were frazzled, and Lisa's even more so. They were met at Tan and Lisa's newly purchased cottage with the smiling faces of their partners, who proudly showed off not a rented tuxedo, but a tailored suit of a deep purple that was a good foil for Tan's native Inuit coloring and would pass muster for formal occasions many years to come.

"Tuxes made her look shorter, for some reason, like it was just too much clothing," Eve explained after Ani kissed her hello.

"I've seen her wear forty pounds of jackets and scarves."

"Not in a wedding party," Eve said.

"Do you want a wedding, darling?" Lisa was explaining her lack of success to Tan and Ani had heard it all. It was far more fun to hold Eve close and look into her smiling, inviting eyes.

"Yes, I do. I decided today. When it will be legal where we live, I want a wedding. And I'm inviting the whole town of North Pole. If you're good, I'll invite you too."

Ani kissed her, which was what the joke deserved. "I always try to be good."

Eve made a gratifying, suggestive noise and Ani pulled her close. In the background she heard Lisa begin the story of the second of their eight shops. Even doubling her budget hadn't helped.

"I might as well make myself a toga out of a sheet," she was saying. "Money doesn't help in the least unless I want to spend thousands on a custom-fitted dress—and wait three weeks."

Rocking Eve slightly, Ani added, "There was one dress that came close, but it made her ass look fat."

Tan shuddered in mock horror as she gave Lisa another hug. Her expressive eyes held deep sympathy for Ani, which Ani appreciated. "We can't have that. Darling, I'd rather you were in a swimsuit than something that profaned your hindquarters."

It made Lisa laugh and relax. Amazing, Ani thought. She knew if she'd said the same thing Lisa would still be chewing her ear about it an hour later.

"Pull over!" Lisa pointed at an ordinary New England house—two-story A-frame, set back from the street, small garden around a single oak tree and a narrow driveway leading to the back. "Yard sale!"

"We're not going to find a wedding dress at a yard sale."

Ani was tempted to keep driving but a space opened up right in front of the next house on the street. She was already annoyed at having taken the wrong exit from the latest roundabout and finding herself on this one-way side street. If that damned GPS box told her she was "off route" one more time, it was going to be airborne out the window. Lisa was far too frazzled to drive, or so she said. It was easier to order Ani to do impossible things in New England traffic when, to Ani, a traffic jam was four cars at a four-way stop.

"There was a big rack of clothes. I have a feeling."

She had to stop. It was not possible to argue with Lisa's "feelings." She had hoped to spend today on the Freedom Trail with Eve, but no, more wedding dress shopping instead. It was already after two and there was no hint of a clam or lobster roll in her future. Eve and Tan had woken up early and been out of the house to beat the commute for the drive to Salem, so Ani hadn't even gotten a smooch and a 'good morning' from Eve. She *always* got a 'good morning' from Eve. Given the long, long winter nights with the sun rising around ten a.m., Eve's 'good morning' was sometimes the only thing that marked a new day.

Tan at least had felt badly about sightseeing without Ani, but she wasn't allowed to see the dress in advance and there was no point to three of them going shopping and leaving Tan on her own. It was Spring Break for the state colleges and her vacation as well. So she and Eve were tromping around the House of Seven Gables, and had probably had something like pumpkin ravioli for lunch or seafood stew with crusty steaming Italian rolls and melted butter and probably chocolate mousse or lemon custard for dessert or found a shop with ice cream cones.

It was at least welcome to get out of the car and into the brisk, crisp air. She couldn't explain it, but the air felt older to her here in New England, like it had brushed against history before mingling through the newly leafing trees. Air in Alaska felt like it had been dancing with Denali before she breathed it in. Also unlike home, wildflowers were everywhere, which she liked, and the sun was out longer, but that was true of just about everywhere. It was only mildly hot—low seventies—but the shade was comfortable to her.

Lisa made a beeline for the clothes rack, seizing and pulling out a white dress. As Ani got closer she saw it wasn't exactly white so much as a pale blue. It was a better choice for Lisa's skin and hair than pure white. It was sort of gauzy and very feminine without being super frilly. She actually liked it.

"The waist is too big." Lisa held it against herself. "But I like the bodice and sleeves. I'm thinking this was a bridesmaid dress, and a pretty nice one."

The sleeves were also appealing to Ani. They would only reach halfway down Lisa's forearm, but they draped so that it appeared the sleeves were gathered and tied with pretty velvet ribbon, leaving a lot of arm exposed. Sexy. But the waist was way too large.

"It's silk and it's only twenty-five dollars," Lisa whispered. "Do you think I could find someone good enough at alterations to do it by day after tomorrow?"

"That seems like a big job. The whole waist would have to come off and go back on, wouldn't it?"

A harried-looking middle-aged woman paused on the other side of the rack. "That's the trouble trying to sell it. I was almost five months along when it was fitted to me."

"I'm getting married on Saturday, kind of in a hurry because our friends are here and we thought, well, why not now instead of this summer?" Lisa's charm was in full force. "But the dress has become the biggest issue. I want to look okay in the photos for the grandkids."

Ani tried to stifle a snort.

"It would really suit you," the woman said. Suddenly she

turned and called, "Mom! Come ovah here!"

Within moments a much older woman, white-haired and sharp-eyed, appeared. "What is it Julie?"

"Could you alter this?" Julie turned to Lisa. "My mom made that dress. She was a seamstress for decades."

"You *made* this?" Lisa clasped the gown to her again. "It's beautiful."

"I can alter it, but how soon?"

"She needs it tomorrow night I'm thinking."

Expert eyes sized up Lisa and the dress. "It would take me all day, stahting now too. Cost probably more than it's worth."

The third generation of the household arrived with a cheery smile under her Boston University ball cap. Ani thought the girl was probably an undergrad. The family resemblance, anchored around long, thin noses and sharp blue eyes, was striking. All saleswoman, she enthused, "That's a great dress."

The mother nodded, but said, "Only if she can wear it, and she can't."

The girl said brightly, "Nana's making me one a lot like it for my wedding this fall."

The grandmother nodded, but said, "Only if you set a date and put a deposit on St. Michael's. I'm not stitching anything until then."

"Nana, that's what the yard sale is for—the deposit." The girl rolled her eyes. Clearly, in her opinion, her grandmother had a terrible memory.

"Not to mention the catering and the bartender and the D.J. and the dance floor you're wanting to pahk in my backyahd."

"It can't be done in time, anyway," Ani added. Her stomach growled loudly—she knew Lisa heard it, but all Lisa did was bump her out of the way.

"I'm a bartender," Lisa said. "I can pour any of the basic stuff. Maybe we can work something out. I'll advise you on what to buy and then tend for your reception and I'll get a dress fitted to me by tomorrow night? Maybe?"

There was a long, considering silence. Then the granddaughter's gaze slid over to her grandmother, pleading like a puppy. A few moments later, far more resigned but equally pleading, the mother's gaze shifted as well.

The grandmother, obviously a woman used to dealing with people, said, "I'd want a contract. I don't want to do all that work and you not show up."

"Done," Lisa said.

Just like that, the grandmother, who introduced herself as Elaine, asked Ani and Lisa inside. Within minutes they were all crowded into the bathroom. Lisa was promptly stripped to her skivvies and measured while Ani wrote out the straightforward terms of the agreement.

And even full of pins the dress clearly flattered and would fit like a charm. Naturally, Ani thought, because it's for Lisa and Lisa had a feeling and I *still* don't have any lunch headed my way.

The door to the bathroom opened and another white-haired woman stuck her head in. "Lainie, what are you doing?"

Mouth full of pins, Elaine said, "What does it look like?"

"Guess I'm going for grub on my own."

"You've managed that for the past forty years even without me along sometimes."

"You want the usual?"

"Lee, I'm busy here. Yes, the usual if you're going to Murphy's."

"Got it." The door closed.

Lisa, who obviously didn't have a stomach clanging at her for something to eat, said, "Tan is going to love this dress. She loves everything I wear, but this is going to knock her eyes out."

"Just what a bride wants on her wedding day." Elaine gave

Ani a considering look in the mirror and went back to pinning the dress, a satisfied smile now on her face.

Ani, without consulting Lisa because she could make decisions by herself, opened the door and peered into the adjacent sitting room. Lee was just putting her wallet into the back pocket of well-worn jeans. "Can I come with you? I'm starving and my so-called friend doesn't seem to care."

"We're going to be here a while," Elaine announced with amazing clarity in spite of the pins. "Go have a pint with my girl."

Ani grinned at Lee.

Lee grinned back as she scrubbed her short, thick hair. "You like baseball?"

I hope I have her hair when I grow up, Ani thought. "Sorry, there aren't any pro teams in Alaska so I don't know much. Do you like glaciers?"

Lee blinked. "Can't say I've thought about it. You drink beer?"

Lisa answered for Ani. "Like a fish."

Lee spoke loud enough that her voice carried. "I didn't know fish drank beer."

Ani snorted. "I like a cold one now and again, sure." She followed Lee outside. Amazingly, Lisa had nothing more to say, or if she did Ani could no longer hear her.

Two days later they took separate cars to the courthouse. Tan and Eve had a twenty-minute start with the task of establishing a place in the registrar's line. An early morning shower had given way to scattered clouds, and the occasional burst of sunshine was lovely, Ani thought.

They had taken photos of Lisa in her gown as soon as Tan and Eve had left. Avoiding the wet leaves and grass had been achieved by Ani wielding a beach towel whenever necessary—which meant Lisa's dress was dry and Ani's black trousers were soaked. Ani thought it silly to preserve the "don't see the bride in the dress until the last moment" rule but Tan was equally insistent. Ani knew hers was not to question, etc. and had snapped pictures of Lisa shaded under the pear tree, daintily perched on the garden bench and looking radiant in front of the ivy-covered trellis.

She and Eve had ordered hers-and-hers iris corsages for both of the brides, and Lisa's was beautiful against the pale blue of her dress. Her hair was down around her shoulders where the clever Elaine had stitched a little more of the shoulder seam closed to hide the very necessary straps on the very necessary bra. Nevertheless, as they left the courthouse parking lot, the attractive curves of Lisa's bronzed shoulders drew admiring glances which Ani knew Lisa was aware of but of course Lisa did not acknowledge. She was *such* a prom queen.

Tan and Eve were waiting on the steps with Tan's grin already announcing that all had gone well so far. Tan's eyes weren't knocked out, but it wasn't for want of trying. Lucky woman in love, Ani thought, just like I am.

Eve was slender and refined in a navy blue pant suit. Small, but genuine diamond chip earrings, Ani's last anniversary gift to her, winked in the spring sunlight. The violet blouse lit up her eyes, though Ani liked to think that was due to her arrival.

Lisa smiled, looking impossibly demure. "What do you think?"

Tan gazed down at her as she descended the steps. "If I tried to describe my feelings at the sight of you in that dress we'd be here all day before I even got to *beautiful*. *Beautiful* doesn't even begin to cover it."

"Marry me?" Lisa held out a hand and Tan wrapped it in her own.

"How about right now?"

Lisa paused, considering. "Well, that's a gorgeous suit you have on, and you look incredibly handsome and wonderful, so why waste it? Okay, I'll marry you right now."

Eve caught Ani rolling her eyes and gave her a look that said she needed to be a little more indulgent.

"Whatever," Ani muttered under her breath.

They waited only a few minutes more for the clerk, and Tan and Lisa walked away with their license, witnessed by Ani and Eve. That was kind of cool, Ani thought. She'd never really thought about the officialness of marriage since she'd not had the option available to her. The license, with an official seal and raised lettering and witnessed signatures, was heavier than it looked. If she thought about the fact that she couldn't get that significant piece of parchment where she lived she would get angry and it just wasn't the day for that. She thought instead of the lovely dinner they had planned when the ceremony was over.

But it wasn't hard to notice that Lisa was just about every boy's picture of a Playmate, stunning in her curves, hair, smile…sexy to the very end of her toenails. Male gazes followed her across the lobby. Ani was amused when those looks transferred to the lucky fellow on her arm. Every single one of them blinked, looked at the less feminine but still obviously female Tan again, then got a "Oh man, I couldn't have her if I wanted to, even." *Got that right, fellas*, Ani wanted to tell them, *She is Not for You.*

Eve gave her a curious look and Ani realized she was grinning. "Tell you later," she whispered as they moved into the queue for ceremonies. After a short wait a woman in black slacks and a flowered red blazer introduced herself as the justice-of-the-peace and took them to a small room for vows. Ani had expected a plain administrative type room, but there was some seating for spectators and the wall was decorated with a quilting pattern of gold rings that Ani thought was romantic.

This was the part of weddings that Ani tended to find hokey. All that dearly beloved stuff. But their officiating justice offered them a selection of vows, one of which was simple and to the point. Tan chose that one. After more deliberation Lisa agreed as well. Finally, the ceremony began.

Standing behind the brides, Ani was close enough to Eve to link fingers. She gave them a squeeze and Eve returned a brilliant, teary smile. What was it with weddings and tears? It was a happy day, after all, wasn't it?

"…To be my lawful wedded wife…" Tan intoned seriously.

It was all going smoothly. Ani wasn't disconcerted when Eve's tears spilled over. She had a tissue ready and offered it even before Eve got one out of her own pocket. Lisa really did look radiant, she mused. She'd always wondered why people said that about brides, but there was a palpable glow.

"…Till death do us part," Tan finished.

The justice turned to Lisa. "Repeat after me. 'I…'"

Lisa's eyes shimmered with tears. Ani surreptitiously took a photo, which turned out to be a good thing because Lisa opened her mouth and no sound came out. Then she burst into full-on, chin-quivering, drop-spurting tears.

It took several tries before Lisa even got "I, Lisa" out of her mouth, then she sobbed her way through her vows as the justice patiently waited. Tan looked as if she was about to cry as well, and Eve was sniffling almost as loud as Lisa. Their emotions were already infecting the wedding party that was waiting to use the room next, with the grandmothers and mothers involved dabbing madly at their eyes while the groom cleared his throat and kept his gaze on his feet.

Don't cry, Ani thought, because if you do somehow it'll be your fault. So she didn't cry and in spite of the incredible temptation, she didn't take a photo of Lisa's mascara smeared face and smudged lipstick. She wanted to, real bad. Would she ever get some credit for her restraint? Unlikely.

They'd chosen a lesbian-owned café in Waltham for an early dinner, planning to move on to a nightclub that was hosting a girls' dance party for the final Saturday of Spring Break. At the café door they were greeted by the smiling chef-owner. When Lisa began to explain the reason for their attire and celebration, the owner just smiled and led them to a sequestered table for four.

Lisa stopped dead at the sight of pale blue and deep purple ribbons twined together and draped over the chairs. A lovely bouquet of irises and baby blue carnations graced the table.

"Oh my goodness," she said. She immediately turned to Eve. "This was your doing, I just know it."

"Ani's idea," Eve said.

"Yeah," Ani said. "I'm good for something, you know."

Lisa gave her a nonplussed look, then broke into a grin and enveloped her in a big hug. "Okay, I love you. Don't know what I'd do without you."

Tan coughed.

Very pleased by the hug, Ani gave her a push toward Tan. "She's stuck with you now."

Tan, ever unflappable, nodded solemnly. "She is stuck with me too."

Ani ushered Eve into her chair and planted a small kiss behind her left ear, right in that warm, tender spot that wasn't quite neck and not really throat. It was so delicious she did it on the other side as well. "Stuck with me?"

A dancing look of desire and promise was the answer she got, and Ani was glad Tan and Lisa were retiring for the night to a fancy hotel, leaving the cottage to her and Eve. She was certain they would find a way to pass the time. And sometime after sunrise Eve would roll over to snuggle into her arms and say, "Good morning."

And her day would start, the way it should always start, in Eve's arms.

Wild Things

Published:	1995
Characters:	Faith Fitzgerald, professor and historical biographer
	Sydney Van Allen, lawyer and politician
Setting:	Chicago, Illinois

The Sixth is Serendipity

Losing Faith

(15 years)

It is quite one thing to be a professor of history and quite another to be history, I wrote in my journal. I paused to look out at the darkening sky and rising lights, pondering the view from the top floor of the Omni Park West.

It was beautiful and ethereal. But it had been chosen because there was no direct line of sight from any other structure in Manhattan into this or the other rooms that shared this side of this floor. It had been three days since I'd ceased to see the view for its wonder. Instead, when I looked, I heard in my head the Secret Service pronouncement: sniper safe.

The wall was open between the Presidential Suite and the Junior Presidential Suite, where I was. The immense combined common space was crammed with folding tables that were in turn encrusted with laptops. Every chair was occupied with a frazzled aide and they were all talking on their cell phones. The conversation was nothing but fragments. In this world, no one ever finished a sentence unless they were being recorded.

For once, the press detail had been sequestered. There was heavy politicking going on.

"But if Jefferson won't see us tonight, that means we're screwed and the old—"

"I don't care what your poll says, our polls are national, not regional, and there's no question that—"

"Look here, you can't just ask for confirmation and not tell me who's asking, I won't—"

The voices overlapped in a fury of purpose. Just past this fountain of energy sat my lover, Sydney Van Allen, looking every inch the Ice Queen she'd been dubbed many years ago. Not caring to mimic the red jacket trend for female political candidates she was as usual dressed in cream and ivory tones, from fitted linen trousers to the cashmere sweater that was also threaded with a bright aquamarine. Her much discussed shoes were today classic, elegant Magli pumps as faithfully reported on sydneysshoeblog.com.

I knew she heard it all, but she reacted to nothing. Like everyone else she was waiting on Senator Randall Mayhurst Jefferson's decision. Who could blame Jefferson for savoring his role as one of the most powerful men in the world—if only for a few hours?

I heard someone ask, "Is Faith here?"

I turned, gestured. The frantic aide rushed up. I recognized her—she was the one assigned to wardrobe. I got the usual question.

"Has the candidate finalized her attire for the convention's afternoon session tomorrow?"

"Senator Van Allen knows."

Wide eyes. "I can't ask her."

I pointed. "She's right over there. She doesn't look busy." Use your eyes, I wanted to say, and ask yourself if that woman needs my help dressing. Sydney had impeccable taste that came with inherited wealth. Some pundits used photos of her closet, bills from boutiques in Milan and the shoe blog mania to portray her as a silver-spoon elitist. She had inherited hundreds of millions. Wearing Wal-Mart jeans would be patronizing, which the same pundits would then also criticize. So she kept her style, and donned safety gear over it in factories and mines. Workers did give her a wide berth—at first. But when she listened to them with her whole being, asked questions that said she understood the limitations of wages and worker safety regulations, the people she talked to walked away feeling as if they'd been heard by someone who both cared and had a chance to do something about their concerns. I'd seen it happen many times—it was her magic.

The aide tiptoed across the crowded, noisy room and I went back to my journal.

I am doubtful that male spouses of female candidates are asked to keep track of their wives' clothing, but this is a tediously routine request for my attention, and one area that Sydney and I have specifically agreed would never be my purview. I am a professor; we are not a species known for our fashion sense.

Resting my wrists on the keyboard support pad, I paused to wonder if my journal was becoming a record of whining. I truly believed that Sydney had an unlimited political capacity, and that she would be an amazing, motivating, galvanizing vice president, should her running mate prevail at tomorrow evening's voting, and the general public's only ten weeks from now. She was the only woman in contention for the job of vice president among any of the political parties this election. If she was sworn in little baby lesbians everywhere would know they too could be a heartbeat from the highest office in the

United States.

We'd not spent more than a night in our Chicago apartment in over four months.

We'd not been alone together in over eight months—but then my definition of *alone* meant no security posted directly outside our hotel room door. Not yet a candidate for high office, Sydney's security detail was still private, but they had been receiving advice from the Secret Service ever since the first "routine" death threats. I was supposed to be used to it by now.

As a historian, I had promised myself I would not censor my journal. Someday it could be part of a presidential archive. Someday, some historian much younger than me would read it. It should not be prettied up, it should not reflect only my best thoughts. If I allowed that to happen I owed a number of students better grades than I had given them.

I was about to resume typing when the scent of Sydney's cologne tickled at my nose. It was custom-made for her and always made me think of sunshine on warm linen.

Leaning back in my chair, I stretched my hand over my shoulder, wiggling my fingers in greeting. She took them in her hand and turned me to face her.

"You look so solemn." Her brown eyes, velvet eyes, wrapped me in affection.

"Recording for posterity the inappropriateness of being asked about your wardrobe plans."

"I've told her time and again to always ask me. I'm sorry they see you as the typical wife."

"I mostly am the typical wife," I said. "It's their view of what a typical wife does that I find regressive."

She kissed my forehead—the one public display of affection candidates in her position were really allowed. Politics today, however, meant it was entirely possible a rabid pundit would insist that the unborn child of the aide that was pregnant could be forever damaged by our wanton displays. The wedding rings on our fingers were no shield against people who made millions as professional liars.

I wanted to relax into her. Put my head on her shoulder, tell her a funny story or ask her to go to the movies with me. We'd discuss the choices, air our feelings about the performers, and if we should disagree we'd share a kiss or two to make it all better.

Our disagreements could be spirited. The making up... more so.

I missed that. I missed her.

Perhaps she knew, because she let me lean into her for a long moment, giving me strength. I took it, greedy creature that I am. When she was standing in the convention wings tomorrow evening, waiting for her momentous speech as a woman on the edge of history, I would give every ounce of energy I had back to her.

An aide slammed down a phone and cursed loudly.

"Watch it." David Morrell, the campaign manager, had strict rules about profanity. Between that and Sydney's icy stare, few staffers forgot.

"Sorry. I just spent two hours trying to get Jefferson's calendar and all I'm getting is the runaround. If he's decided which candidate he's going to visit first tonight, he's not saying."

I turned back to my keyboard, but I continued to listen.

Sydney returned to the main room. "Are we so sure it matters that much? Who he sees first?"

"Absolutely," David said. "Whoever it is will be an instant leak to the press, and then the polling will start, right then. If it's us, we could know by six a.m. how it's playing in Peoria."

"If I can't play Peoria, I've no business playing Madison Square Garden tomorrow." Sydney's voice was droll, almost laconic. "Is there any sign of the revision to the section on immigration policy and education statistics?"

"I'll have it for you in about five." I continually forgot that young woman's name. She was good at her job, punching up Sydney's speeches, though all her work then went through the senior speechwriter for the ticket. Isabella? Like the queen? I wasn't sure. I supposed the many years of seeing hundreds of students and never learning their names had ill-trained me for remembering names now. They were all so young, and so earnest.

History is full of stalwart political wives, I wrote. *Or, if not stalwart, competent campaigners and genteel activists for genteel causes. I often feel that with so many specialists I have nothing left to give Sydney that I could do as well as anyone else. There's only one thing I can give that no one else can: love. She has my love, will have all of me if she asks, and can give me all of her, for safekeeping, for loving, for soothing, for sleeping even, and know that I will never falter. No matter how high she climbs I am at the bottom of any fall. She says it's easier to walk a high wire, even risk a trick or two, knowing she can fall.*

Behind me the debate raged about what Jefferson would decide. Two candidates had roughly equal numbers of delegates, but not enough to clinch the nomination. Jefferson had the rest. So he chose the convention winner and in ten weeks would deliver Texas in the general election. He would be owed favors, big favors. A prominent cabinet post, or, if he wanted to relax from the harder work of politics, an ambassadorship. Luxembourg is lovely, I've heard.

Sydney had resumed the chair at the other end of the room, looking calm and collected again. I knew she sat so she wouldn't pace. Her knee was bothering her but I guessed no one saw that but me. At home I'd have brought her a couple of ibuprofen tablets and a half glass of milk. Here, in this fishbowl, candidates were never seen taking pills of any kind.

A flurry and shared intake of breath told me that the

candidate, Governor Frank Pawtucket from the great state of Michigan, had returned.

David must have delivered a quiet update, because the next thing I heard was Frank—whose voice could pierce concrete—asking, "What in hell is he up to?"

Sydney abruptly spoke. "I think this is about me."

"Don't give yourself airs, Syd." I turned in time to see Frank sliding his suit jacket off his broad shoulders. "This is probably about donors and what's being offered to Jefferson even as we speak."

Sydney made a face. "Sure, nobody is wondering if Pawtucket can win with a lesbian as his running mate. Come on Frank, I know the polling hasn't stopped. The more likely you're in, the more people are suddenly faced with the possibility of yours truly." She laughed. "How did Peckerhead put it? Just when we thought the Vice Presidency couldn't be more diminished than it is, they're seriously talking about a lesbo VP?"

Frank and David laughed. Sydney wasn't given to euphemisms, but the pundit in question was, in point of fact, a peckerhead.

"Syd, don't start on that you're-not-worthy meme, okay? You and I see eye-to-eye on all major domestic issues. You've been on the Armed Services Committee for the last four years. You brought a huge chunk of the progressive wing with you. You're the best lesbo for the job."

Aides snickered and went back to their work. Frank and David paced. Sydney sat still as a statue. No word came from Jefferson's camp.

At midnight I went to bed.

In real life, sunrise rarely portends momentous days. I let the curtains fall back over the window and adjusted the desk lamp so it shone only on my keyboard. *No red sunset at morning for politicians to take warning. This morning's sunrise is no different than yesterday's. The sun is yellow, the light is bright, and no one has heard whether Jefferson has gone to visit the other side. His office has not called us either. Sydney's speech commences in a little under twelve hours. We leave for the convention in seven hours. She's to be introduced by the Speaker of the House—but so far no one knows if she'll be introduced as the Senator from the great state of Illinois, or candidate for the next Vice president of the United States.*

I stretched at my desk in our bedroom off the junior of the two suites, not yet ready to be out in the bullpen. Sydney hadn't come to bed until very late and I was letting her sleep, in defiance of her instructions. Beauty sleep, I would tell her.

Turning my head, I studied her profile. She had no need of beauty sleep, not in my eyes. Her short blonde hair was a mess. She'd not taken the time to wash off her make-up, so mascara smeared one cheek. Beautiful, my Sydney, in her moments of imperfection. Human and vulnerable, though only I saw that.

A bustle outside our door was followed by quiet. I was certain that if there was any word from Jefferson, Sydney would be awakened. I envied Sydney her sleep. I wanted to go for a very long walk—ill-advised. The security detail would be stretched too thin if I left the hotel.

I took one last look at Sydney's face in repose. The idea that by the Tuesday after the first Monday in November there was a chance people would call her Madam Vice president was still beyond my comprehension. I understood it purely academically.

I suspected that if I let myself feel anything but historical interest in the process I would be terrified. Deeper than that there were other emotions I would not name. My interest in my journal dwindled and I remembered there had been the aroma of coffee earlier.

To my surprise I found Governor Pawtucket alone in the

bullpen. He looked tired. The breakfast buffet was decimated but there was still coffee.

"Good morning, Dr. Fitzgerald." He was always genial and welcoming with me.

"I think you could call me Faith," I said, not for the first time.

"When you call me Frank."

"That wouldn't be appropriate, sir. You could be my president in ten weeks." I finished adding cream and stirred the result.

"That's not looking likely at the moment."

"No word?"

"Not a peep." He stirred and I realized his large hands were hiding an empty napkin with donut crumbs—a no-no according to Mrs. Pawtucket. "I'm glad we have a few quiet minutes. The kids are all down in the press room."

His affectionate term for the score of aides and interns made me smile. "Peace and quiet is hard to come by." I wondered if he would like me to retreat and give him back his solitude.

"My wife is a huge fan of your books. She eats biographies for breakfast. She loved the book about Queen Isabella."

I knew that about Mrs. Pawtucket. I liked her. She reminded me of myself—a professional woman with a life of her own usurped by her husband's political fortunes. I thought she did better than I at coping. Of course a large part of her energy had always gone to normalizing life for her children. They were now in college. In their married life, the timing of a presidential run this year made a great deal of sense.

I was aware, inappropriately, that Sydney was melted in sleep, her body warm and supple, only twenty feet away from me. If we were quiet…even though we weren't alone…I'd been a fool to leave our bed to brood.

Thinking about sex on a momentous day like this made

me feel frivolous and shallow. But I wasn't the candidate or running mate. For me, no day would be more momentous than the one when Sydney had told me she loved me.

Frank, his intelligent eyes watchful, was expecting an answer. I sat down across from him on one of the uncomfortable, overstuffed chairs and said, "Thank your wife for me. I appreciate any and all readers."

"Where do you think we stand? In history, today?"

I matched his nonchalantly false smile. "History is never contemporary. Only with perspective will we know what today means. It could mean nothing."

He nodded. "I know that—what might today become, then?"

"If Jefferson waits until after the Senator's speech this evening, it could mean nothing."

He smiled, slightly annoyed. "I know that too. So you think there's no potential for today?"

"There's always potential. He could call right now. The history of today isn't ours to make."

"Tell me about it."

I shrugged. "Jefferson makes the history today. Historians will remember, but history itself will remember what came of it—it can be fickle about remembering who made it." Winning the general election, having a successful presidency, building a legacy relevant to the future—yet to be accomplished before history bothered with Jefferson or any of us.

I pushed away why I found that thought comforting. "Reporters will be proclaiming this a history making day. It's their job, in the moment, to suggest that it is."

"Historians are always too late with the facts."

I smiled. "If we weren't we wouldn't be historians."

He set aside his empty coffee cup. "If you were writing history, what would you say?"

A glib response died on my lips. Words I would never say,

never record in my journal, hammered behind my suddenly clenched teeth, waking up the headache I often had from grinding my teeth in my sleep.

I was spared recovering by the noisy return of "the kids." After greetings all around I returned to our room to find the bed empty and telltale steam drifting from the bathroom. With no one to witness, I lifted her still warm pillow to my face and breathed in the memory of earlier days.

Peering through the bathroom mist, I saw she was nearly done. I wondered if I dared join her, clothes and all, if that would bring back my Sydney, the one who had joined me in the shower, ruining a very expensive suit, to tell me she loved me and would not go on living without me. I missed her. I missed her desperately.

The shower door opened and Sydney, with a dollop of suds on her nose, said, "Want to join me?"

My tilted world righted, a little. Decorum be damned. I stripped off my clothes and joined her, the hot spray soaking my hair. Our lips met in a fever. I hadn't locked the door to our suite. If Jefferson called and an aide came looking for us...

Sydney's fingers knew the way into me. Where to pause, where to tease, where to push. The years only improved her certainty. I gasped at the chill of the marble against my back. She kissed me, I bit her lower lip. She said something that was lost in the shower spray and I begged.

It drew a groan from her that spoke of years of desire, of having and *us*. No polish, no mansions, no pretense. Us, hot for each other, incomplete without the very thing that marked us pariahs in some parts of the world. We had always celebrated this, appropriately, with lust and abandon.

There was water in my eyes, her voice deep in my head. My feet slipped. She carried us both, soaking wet, to the bed and had me again, this time in silence, not a word, not a sound. I know my eyes were screaming. The flush on her shoulders was poetry. And her eyes, velvet brown, wrapped me close in her liquid fire.

"Legs shaky?"

She nodded at me in the bathroom mirror. "So are yours."

I smiled at my reflection as I tried to recreate this morning's hair before someone realized I'd been in the shower again. "Yes and thank you."

"You're welcome," she said lightly, then her smile faded. "The oddest thing happened when I woke up this morning." She turned to face me. "I didn't know who I was."

My eyebrows skyrocketed. "Really?"

"I mean—I knew. But this room was so foreign and I couldn't remember how I got here. I knew my name, but I kept thinking that I didn't know who I was."

I touched her arm in concern. "Syd, are you okay?"

"Yes. Now I am. When I saw you I remembered." She rested her cheek against mine, not spoiling either of our make-up with kisses. "I know."

I slipped my arms around her. "Who are you?"

"Yours."

I blinked back tears. I suspected that wasn't the only answer, but I accepted that it was definitely part of it. Each of us was separately successful, and our work had little overlap. But we defined each other, in part, inseparable, having each given up pieces of ourselves to gain even more.

"Senator? Dr. Fitzgerald?"

We sprang apart, though we were fully clothed.

Sydney called, "Not quite ready—what is it?"

"Jefferson just asked for a meeting with the Governor. We're first."

Polls were already rolling out as the media-blog-cycle went viral with the news that Jefferson had chosen the Pawtucket ticket to negotiate with first. Would he ask for legislation guarantees for his constituency? Would he make a bid for a cabinet post?

My heart rate had gone up and wouldn't calm. This was it. This was the last eight months of public speaking, travel, photo ops, ever since Pawtucket had made the novel choice to announce his entire ticket and staff early. He wanted Americans to know what they were going to get, no surprises, no key players unvetted by the press. No one had known then that Jefferson would have the final say.

David snapped his cell phone shut. "He's on his way back."

"That didn't take long," Sydney said.

David appeared crestfallen. "No. No, it didn't. That's not good."

I would not let myself feel. I stayed on the knife's edge, dulled the whirlwind by remembering Sydney with me on the bed not fifteen minutes earlier.

The elevator ride for Frank Pawtucket probably seemed longer to him than the few minutes did to me, and I lived several years during them. Years of curling up with Sydney in our Chicago sanctum, getting used to the many privileges and minor disadvantages of her wealth, then her political position. The year of campaigning when she left the Illinois statehouse for Congress, then years of adapting to part-time life in D.C. It seemed that the quickness of the meeting meant those years were over.

I would not let myself feel.

The door finally opened. Frank's escort faded to the side and he came in with a heavy tread. I wondered where Mrs. Pawtucket was—probably grooming children and their spouses, making sure all looked perfect for the cameras when they emerged from the hotel. She was better at this than I was. Of course, Sydney's parents, her brother and his family, her many relatives also in public office, needed no help from me to look right for the cameras. My own family stayed home. They always had.

The man looked like he could use a hug.

He glanced around the room and gave a wan smile. "Thank you, everybody. I couldn't have asked for better."

"What happened?" David leaned against one of the tables, pale.

"His price was too high."

"What was it?" That was Sydney, moving from my side into Frank and David's equal line of sight.

"Too high," Frank said again. He looked every day of his sixty-one years.

"Give it to him," she said.

"No. That's out of the question."

I had the feeling that Sydney knew exactly what the price was.

"That decision is partly mine." She crossed her arms.

David gaped. "He wouldn't have the balls for that!"

Sydney gave him a droll look. "We're talking about Jefferson, the biggest little ego on the planet. He lost this race—didn't even come in second. He came in a lousy third. Now he's a spoiler. And he wants the world."

David was shaking his head. "No, it would destroy every message we've been crafting for over a year."

"I don't think so," Sydney said. "We are a coalition. If we can't show flexibility and inclusion, a willingness to broaden our tent stakes, then we've been lying." She turned her head to give Frank a long look.

"No," he said.

"Give it to him. Call him now and give it to him. I'll go with you. Or we all go home. Everybody who worked for you, who went into their local machine and got people who never agree

70

to sit down and talk for decency and sanity and the strength of compromise—they all go home. If we don't succeed, no one will try it our way again. And I think our way is the only way our country is going to survive against fearmongering for profits and lies for news."

The sunset had not foretold this momentous day. I was watching it unfold and as Sydney and Frank left together, I didn't know what I had seen.

The convention floor was deafening. The excitement at Sydney's impending speech had awakened the crowd after a dull procedural afternoon. The word had spread that Jefferson had decided, and that his camp was in contact with the Pawtucket camp, indicating his probable support in the voting later tonight. Crazy convention schedule, arranged around television and momentum. If Pawtucket had Jefferson's support, they could take the nomination with a single vote of acclamation, in prime time, with Sydney's speech the run-up to the call for a vote. Tomorrow night, for his big speech, Pawtucket wouldn't be campaigning for his party, he would be campaigning to the country. It was the scenario the networks wanted, that the image consultants wanted.

The music was building to a crescendo as it segued from "Chicago" to "New York, New York." Sydney's mother took my hand. I'd explained to all the Van Allens how it was going to unfold. Her father had said, finally, "Why am I surprised? It's so like her."

There was so much glitter falling that I wondered they would have any left for tomorrow, when Pawtucket accepted. The ceiling was heavy with balloons in nets. Tonight the balloons were all the colors of the rainbow. Tomorrow, nothing but red, white and blue.

The Van Allens and I were all arranged in prime box seats. Visible to cameras from around the world, I knew that at any moment my image would be on televisions across the country, and they would label me "Dr. Faith Fitzgerald, Senator Van Allen's wife." Fifteen years ago we had thought just the whisper of my existence in Sydney's life would kill her political chances forever.

Not then. Maybe now. History would tell.

I knew that transcripts of her speech would be available, so I listened with my heart. Even though we were not that far away, she looked tiny on the big stage, but regal. The big screen behind her showed her tall and assured, and the audio carried her voice realistically. At times soft with passion, it also rose in fervor. She paused and the glimmer of tears were real, when she noted the tragedy of flooding in the Everglades and resurgent traces of oil rising with tidal action, back into the life of the Gulf Coast. I heard the laser-point of her resolve to champion an effective, permanent response to climate change before Florida was underwater.

Then she spoke of politics. Too true, the adage that like sausage, if you loved politics you should never learn how laws are made.

"I came into politics when we talked to each other. When I would think about a change I wanted to see enacted and find a counterpart on the other side of the aisle, and we talked over the issues and found where we agreed. It was a time when we gave up what we wanted and took what we could have, knowing we could talk again another day, and that was how progress was made. We all grew to understand each other better. And often, we made good law. I've watched those days die, and wondered if it was time for me to get out. Then I met Frank Pawtucket."

From here I couldn't really see her eyes, but I could imagine them. I knew there was not the least shadow of regret.

She would not look back. It wasn't her way.

If the cameras caught Faith's mother wiping her eyes, they would assume they were tears of pride. They'd be right, for the wrong reasons.

I recognized the cue of her final, hastily composed paragraph, coming after two minutes of praise for Governor Pawtucket and his inclusive style of coalition and compromise. It had worked in Michigan. It could work for all of us.

"I agree with Frank Pawtucket. We are twin political children of very different mothers. And that is why I am withdrawing my name from consideration as vice president and instead nominating Randall Mayhurst Jefferson for that office. Our party and our goals do not need people who agree in lockstep. We need reasoned challenge, rational debate and different points of view."

Over the rising murmur of disbelief and discontent, she continued. "I was proud to be part of the negotiation to bring this change to our platform, and I am even more proud of the way the staff handled the change, and realized how much stronger this makes us. For years we've listened to people painting willingness to compromise as weakness instead of inspiration. Our ticket—your ticket—offers you a broad spectrum of ideas and hope that aren't born in expediency, but were forged when Randall Jefferson walked with southern family farmers and marched with miners in West Virginia."

The rest of her words washed around my ears in clear blue conviction. For her, it wasn't spin. Their hope had always been about changing the way politics were conducted so that something got done. I knew she would go on campaigning for the ticket. The restless crowd would quiet. They would listen.

The grace with which she stepped aside and the sheer energy she gave to Jefferson's nomination made me proud. I was so often proud of her, and just as often awed by her astuteness and generosity and willingness to live her convictions. Being outrageously wealthy helped, no doubt, but money hadn't built that spine of steel.

I didn't really like Jefferson much, but then I didn't know him. Sydney was in her second hour of briefing him on the machine she'd put in place and the staff roles that would open up tomorrow for his own people. I had retired to our suite, but left the door open. My tiny laptop in front of me on the desk, I was thinking how to begin describing what had happened today. Eventually, how it had all happened wouldn't be more than a blip in history. Only students of campaigns would recall it when we were all long gone.

No doubt some advisors will say she's been duped into playing the part of the always sacrificing woman. That she's betrayed feminism, her own constituents and little girls everywhere. In time I'm sure she will speak to that. I have a lot to think over as well. What I know is that she acted in the only way she could and still be who she is. She is a woman. She can't have made anything but a woman's decision.

I hesitated, realized I was censoring myself, but still, I turned my thoughts from the gamut of emotions I had felt—those I would not name this morning, and those I would not name now.

Anyone who dismisses her now as having shot her political wad is wrong. History says so, and I am the number one scholar in the history of Sydney Van Allen. She has closed a door. She will rest. She'll make up the lost time to the people of Illinois who sent her to the Senate. In time, she will open a new door, surprising even me with her choice.

In the meantime, we go home.

She had woken up this morning not knowing who she was. When they had come back from their meeting with Jefferson, she had taken me in her arms, comforting me of all people, and whispered in my ear, "This is who I am."

I pondered her words, knowing in part she meant she was my wife, my love, that the future held me. But I also knew she meant the practicality of stepping aside. The choice was give Jefferson the nod or end the dream she believed in because she didn't get to be a leader. She was not an I-win-at-all-costs person. If winning for everybody meant sacrifice from her—that was who she was, always had been and always would be.

I am so proud—

I stopped there. It was true.

If I continued I would be censoring history. Pride, though it brimmed in me, was the least of my feelings.

This morning I had been so afraid of losing our life forever to history. But I'd also been angry with her for risking all that we had built together for each other, for changing us so much. It was disloyal to feel it, unsupportive to think it. I believed in her dreams. We were inseparable and her dreams became mine, but the deeper we were in this particular dream the more I wanted no part of it. It was wrong to be angry with her—she had given me the power to say no.

And known that of course I wouldn't use it. This morning, under it all, I had been frozen with helpless rage I could never let out.

My hands were shaking. From fear and anger, I had been catapulted to joy. She had held me tight, comforting *me* after announcing she had ceded the nomination to Jefferson, and all I had felt was a resounding joy. We could go home. Deliriously happy, I also felt like a traitor.

She had become the embodiment of sacrifice and service, of graciousness and intelligent passion, and here I was selfishly glad it had come to nothing. I knew she would do something else, that it would stretch us, and test me again. But there was no way I was letting history know that I loved a wild eagle with both of my feet stuck in the mud.

I had no awareness that I was weeping into my hands until I smelled Sydney's cologne.

She pulled me into her arms, shushing me like a child. "It's going to be okay."

"I know," I mumbled.

"My parents want to have lunch tomorrow."

"Yes, please."

She rocked me for a while. I calmed enough to marvel at how serene she was. Finally, she said, "It didn't show."

"What didn't show?" I arched back to look into her face.

"How relieved you were."

I tried to deny it for about two seconds, but stopped. I was stunned that she'd known and then thought that *of course* she had known.

"This morning when I woke up, and for a moment I didn't know who I was, I realized you weren't there, in my head. You have been there every morning for all these years. My first thought. I've always told you that and whether you believed me or not, it was true. This morning I had to consciously recall you, touch my wedding ring like a totem, and ground myself in reality. I don't think I knew until then how scared I was at what this job would take from me. It was going to change us and I am not sure for the better. I'm not ready to fade into my elder years—and I'm not ready for our love to do that either."

I had no capacity to speak. I tried to look my truth at her, all of my guilt and lack of faith, my selfishness.

"Oh, sweetheart." She cupped my sodden face. "I've suspected for weeks that I would have to step aside. I was ready to make that choice. That's the truth. But it is equally true that when I did it, the loss I felt gave way to relief. If I had to—and I know if *you* had to—we could spend four or eight years not going on dates because that's flaunting our lifestyle, not giving each other gifts because that's flaunting my wealth, you not doing research tours because that's being Marie Antoinette on the people's dime. I know, darling, that you would do that for me."

I nodded. I knew that I would have academically distanced myself until I had no feeling left so that no one—including me—knew how much I hated it. Distanced myself so far that my love for Sydney would also strain…even break. "Now it's unlikely we will have to."

"I think I have a different destiny. Rather, I'm willing to embrace a different destiny. But I won't endanger us again. Not like that."

She pulled me close again, and her voice broke. "We get to go home."

Our roles reversed, I cradled her. Sniffing in her ear, I finally said, "I really don't think we should tell anyone how happy we are."

"This isn't the end," she said.

"That's the best part. And we get to go home."

All the Wrong Places

(Bella After Dark Erotic Romance)

Published: 2004
Characters: Brandy Monsoon, resort fitness instructor
                Tess Carson, resort fitness instructor
Setting: Gulf Coast, Florida

Sweet Fifteen, and ready to grow up

Cruising Solo

(3 years)

"Brandy! Can you help me get these cases to the lounge?"

I turned back from my errand to check yesterday's sales with the Riviera Deck Gift Shop manager. Mel, who was an experienced jill-of-all-trades for the tour company, appeared to be in the midst of her roadie duties. The rolling amplifiers brought on board to boost the sound systems for the musical acts weren't that heavy, but I'd learned yesterday that they were awkward. When our cruise ship made one of its odd jolts the amps wanted to roll one way while the deck tilted another. Add to that some tight corners where passenger traffic was routed around lounges and it wasn't easy for one woman to manage, even one as strong as Mel.

"How's the busman's holiday so far?" Mel put one stocky

shoulder to the back of the amp again and I steadied it from the other side.

"I'm loving it. I just wish my girlfriend hadn't broken her ankle. She'd be loving it too."

"At least you got a cabin to yourself." She grunted as the amp hung up on a slight roll in the carpeting.

I wasn't happy with the empty bed at night. "Ship to shore costs a fortune, doesn't it?"

"Not all that bad," Mel said. "But on our wages it is."

I'd already blown most of my spending money on a beautiful necklace of Venetian glass for Tess's birthday. I couldn't resist it, and I'd missed her so much at our first port-of-call. We'd imagined having just an hour to ourselves to take a gondola ride, but a broken floor tile had other plans. The brief stints with the Internet hookup available when we were in port would have to do.

Mel grappled to keep control of the amp but I caught it before it ran into the steel wall of the exterior hull—the amp was going to be worse for it. "I know why we don't have two sets of these, but moving them from venue to venue is a royal pain."

I averted my eyes from the sight of Mel's rippling biceps. She was about my height but probably carried twenty pounds more muscle—a fine figure of a woman in an A-shirt and shorts. When I'd met her my first thought had been "power butch" and that had proven quite accurate. She also liked to play, if the gossip during the staff lunch was anything to go by. There had been a time when I'd have issued her an invitation or accepted one in a heartbeat.

We finally muscled the amp into the lounge and went back for the second one. Once it was in place the rock band's sound woman took over and Mel and I took a moment to catch our breath. Just as we were leaving, two of the musicians passed us, one saying to the other, "Tuesday night—but invitation only."

The other answered, "Oh, I have my eye on someone to invite already, if I can wait that long to do her."

"I wonder how I could get an invitation to *that* party," Mel said to me as the lounge door closed behind us.

The image of Mel and the heavy metal girls all having a really hot time left me feeling a bit weak in the knees. Tess would laugh—the older I got the more I understood her cat scratch fever hormones. My kitty was in major need.

Mel was regarding me with that mixed expression of cool interest and playful impishness I knew so well from the many times I'd had the same expression. Before I'd left on this trip, Tess, her ankle wrapped in that damned heavy cast, had said, "As long as you come back home to me, I don't care if you have some fun. I don't own your body or your brain, Brandy. Just your heart and your future. Don't do anything that'll cost me either one."

Thankfully, before Mel could actually start the conversation I could tell she was considering, I recalled my original errand.

"Polly wants to know how the CD sales went yesterday. If you see her, would you tell her I got slightly delayed?"

Mel nodded and headed aft while I went up a flight of stairs to the shopping concourse. There were times I forgot I was on a ship, but then there would be a slight hesitation in the rise or fall to remind me. Tess would love the stores, even if we couldn't afford anything in them. There was a turquoise bikini in one window that reminded me vividly of the one she wore for sunbathing, the very one that I had removed many, many times so I could worship the unbronzed parts of her.

The gift shop manager had the previous day's sales records all ready. I glanced down the list and could see that all of the artists had sold a few CDs, but I had no idea if the numbers were strong or lackluster. I hoped Polly would explain and I'd get a chance to show I had a brain for this sort of thing. Tess and I had hopes of joining the Ladies on Vacation Enterprises staff, so we'd plotted to use a week's vacation from our Club Sandzibel resort duties to work this cruise. If they hired us permanently, we could settle into an apartment of our own instead of the two studios Club Sandzibel allotted us. The work was tiring and the days were long, but it was all very fun so far.

By the end of the day I was exhausted in a good way. I'd also overheard a fairly noisy couple having a tryst in the fitness room restroom, which brought back a lot of fond memories. Then there was the couple losing their clothes on the way to their stateroom. They caught me looking and did not seem to mind. After the late night comedy act finished I swear the ship levitated on the lust endorphins alone as the corridors slowly emptied and the guests found warm beds for the night. In some cases, I was certain, the beds they found were not their own.

Feeling sorry for myself, I sat in my stateroom and tried not to miss Tess. I was perfectly capable of arranging some fun—that is if everyone on the prowl hadn't already been claimed—but I was pretty tired. No energy for conversation and flirting at that level.

I decided that a quick tryst with my vibrator might be just the thing and claimed it from the dresser drawer. A search for the nearest outlet to the bed only increased my frustration level. The bargain cabins where staffers stayed were so small there was just one power outlet, in the bathroom, which was so tiny there wasn't even room enough to lie on the floor. Mel had joked that the shower stalls were converted coffins.

And, dang it, I had never mastered the art of having a full-blown, knee-shaking, muscle-clenching orgasm standing up. Twenty minutes later I had ascertained that there was no miraculously appearing extension cord in my suitcase. The corridor outside was empty of any other human beings, let alone one with an extension cord slung over one shoulder.

I was tired and cranky and no longer in the mood to let my vibrator have its way with me.

I went to bed and it took nearly fifteen minutes to fall asleep.

Monday. The home of the Olympic Games. Herding women onto the little boats called tenders to ferry them to shore because the ship was too large to dock. Answering the same question two hundred times. Herding women into the shade, herding them onto shuttles and greeting every minute of the day with a big smile and endless energy. By the time I got off the very last tender back to the ship Polly had already thanked me twice for my help, and praised my quick thinking when a guest had abruptly succumbed to heat stroke. I hoped she remembered I was the one with a girlfriend, as ideal an employee as I was, who had broken her ankle two days before our planned flights. I was playing it low key for now, but I wasn't planning to leave for home without pigeonholing her and giving her the full Brandy and Tess credentials.

Sweaty and tired, and off-duty for the rest of the night, I bumped into Mel on the way to my cabin. She too had been herding women all day and looked as tired as I felt.

"Want to get dinner to go and eat somewhere far away from the guests?"

"Sure," I said easily.

We did just that too. Then, feeling like recalcitrant children, we snuck into the kitchen and helped ourselves to some of the savories and sweets prepared for the pastry extravaganza. I left with an admiring backward glance at beautiful 3-D swans made from phyllo dough and glistening with sugar. A dozen multi-tiered cakes frosted in rainbow colors hadn't yet been cut. But the cinnamon and chocolate puff I'd swiped was light as a feather and filled with a rum-flavored custard—tasty enough to have me licking my fingers.

Mel had that look again as we leaned against the railing and watched the ship splitting the sea dozens of feet below us. "You can tell me to take a hike," she began.

I shrugged. "My girlfriend and I have an understanding."

"Which is?"

"I can be borrowed." If she was here, I didn't add, there wasn't a chance in hell I'd want anyone else. But Tess wasn't here. So maybe for one night I could be the old Brandy.

Mel laughed. "I like that way of looking at it. I'm not the stealing sort. But I don't mind borrowing."

I pulled the bandeau off my hair and let the wind finish ruining it. The damp air only made it more curly and tomorrow morning I'd have some serious work ahead of me.

"You're the first white girl I've ever seen with hair that kinky." Mel touched it briefly and then caressed my neck lightly.

My nipples tightened in response. The old Brandy was very close to the surface now and I wondered what it would feel like to go down on Mel and if she liked having every furl and ripple between her legs thoroughly explored. Or would she want it hard and fast? Was she a butch who liked to be touched? Or was she stone and wanting to spend the night pleasuring me?

I shook suddenly with a feeling of being unleashed. I loved sex and had always enjoyed a new partner. Exploring women, learning them, had for years been one of the highlights of my life. Women are simply the *best*. And here was one ready to play with me, more butch than any I'd ever been with, and I was quite certain there would be more than one new experience with her.

In the three years I had been with Tess we'd had our understanding about borrowing. Mostly it was a recognition that while we wanted to be all the other ever needed if in some circumstances that just wasn't the case, talking about unmet needs and how they might be fulfilled was better than doing anything behind the other's back. Tess had been the one who pointed out that expecting our bodies to never change and our self-knowledge to be static was unrealistic. Certainly her self-knowledge had evolved and that was why she was with me and not a guy. I didn't expect her to never change. I did expect her to want me to be part of those changes.

Given that we worked and lived side-by-side, it wasn't surprising that neither of us had taken advantage of the okay-to-be-borrowed agreement. Any way that we might be changing, such as my strong hormonal drive that I still said I'd caught from her, we'd adapted to together. Here I was, however, eager to be with someone else. Thinking that the experience would be something to tell Tess about. Wondering if the telling would get us in the raunchy mood we both relished.

Mel pulled me into her embrace. The kiss was very nice, and suggested that there could be real heat and real play. "I have a roommate," she said, "so if you'd like, we could go to your cabin."

"It would be a shame to waste it."

"I could pick up a few things from my cabin on the way."

I was about to suggest an extension cord, if she had one, when she cupped my face and kissed me again, harder this time. My skin was tingling as I leaned into her. All that muscle and strength was feeling very, very good to me.

One hand slipped under the waistband of my shorts, gripping my hip.

And I had the thought I could not ignore: *Tess didn't touch me quite like that.*

And then I realized the woman kissing me wasn't Tess. Of course she wasn't. I knew that. It was Mel.

Who wasn't Tess.

She touched me, kissed me and my body responded, no doubt about it. But my infernal brain kept thinking her fingers would move there, or her tongue would touch here, because that was how Tess touched me. Tess who knew my body now better than I did. Tess who possessed every key there was to me.

Fuck a duck, I hate having a brain.

Mel let go of me and gave me a puzzled look. "Are you sure about this?"

"Actually, I'm not." Mel was very nice and I didn't want to hurt her feelings, but only the truth was going to suffice. "You'd just be a stand-in for my girlfriend. I'm sorry."

"I don't care. I get the feeling you are a really fun time."

"I think you probably are too. But…" The truth was inescapable. Morosely, I admitted it. "I love my girlfriend. And while parts of me want you, all of me is only going to be happy with her."

She took my refusal with good grace. I suggested there was plenty of time to cruise the folk singer's show or the late night dance scene. She left me at the railing with a cheery smile and I was fairly certain that the rest of the week wouldn't be awkward between us because of the last few minutes.

I was most of the way to my cabin when I realized I still needed an extension cord.

Fine, I thought, sitting on my bed, all alone. I was being a good girl. Kisses from Not Tess women were useless. I was an old married woman, settled down, constrained, giving up the happy life of soul-wrenching ecstasy through any and all means by which I could find it. And for what?

For a chick with long arms—I could hear Tess saying that

to me clear as day in my head. I fell back on the bed, ruefully laughing. I gave up the footloose and fancy-free life for a woman who some nights could not get fucked enough and all nights could not hold me enough. For a woman who was generous and kind, thoughtful and wise, hot as a firecracker and, frankly, smarter than I was.

I gave up nights with Not Tesses for breakfasts and brownies and tomorrows *and* hot sex with Tess.

Damn, I wanted an extension cord.

The slam of a nearby cabin door brought me to my feet. Peering out into the corridor I summoned up my courage as the couple walked by my door. "I know this will sound weird, but do you have an extension cord I could borrow? I promise you'll have it back in an hour."

"Sorry, mate," the taller woman said as they paused.

Her cuddly girlfriend added, "We were sort of wishing we'd brought one along ourselves."

"Batteries just don't—"

"Got that right, mate—"

"I would have brought one if we'd…"

We all blushed because we all knew exactly what we meant. They drifted toward the stairwell and I heard someone approaching from the other direction.

"Hi," I said cheerfully. "Do you have an extension cord I could borrow for about an hour?"

"Sure," the little redhead said. "I was ironing something earlier, but now I'm all done."

Ironing? That was a bit freaky, but whatever floats your boat, I wanted to say. I had other plans. I thanked her profusely, promised its prompt return, but she told me not to bother until the next day. My vibrator and I could have a long date.

I skipped back to my cabin, plugged everything in, pulled back the covers and spread myself on the bed.

What I needed was a naughty, hot fantasy. The rock band

party, there was a thought.

Muscles and tattoos, I mused, required a soft, pliable woman...perhaps one shared between the two musicians I'd encountered yesterday with Mel. Her hair in ruins, her body slicked with sweat, she'd mewl with need because the more she had, the more she wanted and in my mind's eye, it was Tess wanting it like that, and there were no musicians, just me. Me and Tess, the way we'd been our first night together, and so many nights since.

A flick of my thumb brought the vibrator to life and the intensity of the sensation curled my toes into the bed. I wanted the perfect moment in my head.

My fingers going into Tess, feeling her quivering welcome, thick with want and savoring the twining croon of her rising moan. The perfect moment... The first time... The last time ... The perfect moment, oh...

The first kiss, the one after that, the last kiss, the next kiss when I got home, oh... Oh my.

There were so many perfect moments that about an hour later I selected a few more. In the morning, I mused sleepily afterward, I could have some more perfect moments before I had to give back the extension cord. There was so many to think about, so many that made my nerves jump, so many...all with Tess. And if I ran out of perfect moments, I could make more with her when I got home.

And then I slept, cradled against the pillow that was a poor substitute for Tess's shoulder and let the ship rock me to sleep.

Lucky 7

(4 years)

Happily getting into the groove of brassy, boisterous, bodacious Las Vegas, I finally felt like I knew my way around our hotel. Nothing in a casino went in a straight line, but then again, I'm not that straight either. On the card table side of the ground floor, I had learned to walk on the left side to avoid the smoking area. In the next vaulted chamber, surrounded by marble columns and opulent fountains, I knew to bear right to avoid the line for the hotel's art museum.

Best of all, I knew exactly how to return to where I'd left Tess playing blackjack. There was something about the colors of this particular casino—the white walls, the blue dealer vests, the deep red leather chairs—that I found relaxing and inviting. I'd played video poker longer than I'd meant to and lost my stake. What did that matter when the card tables stretched out before me and there was Tess, perched on the same barstool, her long legs crossed at the knee?

The dealer was a tall, broad-shouldered black woman who was either a dyke or just really fond of women, because Tess's cleavage was getting plenty of attention. Well, someone would have to be dead and buried not to notice Tess and her luscious girls. There were actually an amazing number of really beautiful women in the casino, but none held a candle to Tess. That didn't mean I didn't look, but they made me feel the same as I did for the statues and art all around me—nice to look at, but not something I wanted to take home with me.

Just in case there was any question, though, I sidled up next to my love with a proprietary air.

"Hi babe. Hit me," Tess said.

I was pretty sure I was the babe, and that the dealer was supposed to do the hitting.

Tess gasped as the six landed on table. She flipped over a ten and a five. "Twenty-one!"

The dealer paid her off and grinned as Tess backed away from the table. "You've had quite a string of good luck. Taking the money and running?"

"I've just paid for our vacation." Tess flipped a chip back to the dealer. "Thanks."

"Thank you." The dealer pocketed the chip with a wink. "You two have a fun evening."

Tess dragged me across the casino to the cashier. "Let's get the cash before I change my mind. I'm lucky tonight."

And you're going to get lucky, I wanted to say, but that would be a cheap joke and I was trying to be more subtle these days. We were now gainfully employed tour guides with the most successful lesbian tour group. Though their clientele could appreciate the occasional really bawdy joke, most preferred a refined sense of humor. I was working on it.

"What shall we do for dinner?"

Tess turned from the cashier with a fistful of hundreds and twenties. She was glowing with her accomplishment. "Well, whatever it is, dinner's on me. And we don't need to go to a cheap buffet now."

"How about dinner in that dark little place on the mezzanine?"

"Sounds delightful," she said. We were on the elevator, holding hands, when she added, "You've got quite the cat in the cream look."

I shrugged, hoping I looked debonair and mysterious, a petite and female version of Cary Grant.

"Okay." Tess caught one of the male passengers looking at us. She gave up one of her mega-wattage smiles. "I'm going to get lucky tonight."

The women behind us spluttered with laughter. I glanced over my shoulder—oh, dykes if they were a day old, and they were. One was no taller than I am, which was welcome, and the other was yet another gorgeous creature, tall and lithe, and about as curvaceous as Tess. I gave the short one a solidarity wink since we were both unquestionably lucky dogs.

The woman winked back as if to say, "Yeah, we both married up, didn't we?"

"Our floor, Marian." With a smile at us both, the taller woman pulled her girlfriend after her into the corridor. "If you're done flirting with the other cute little butch, that is."

"I was not flirting, it was—"

The doors closed and I wondered if I was, in fact, giving off a butch vibe these days. I'd always considered myself on the girly side for butch, though I despised handbags and required pockets in my clothes. I could don a little black dress and heels and not feel the least bit weird. Not that I was going to wear that tonight. I had other plans. I supposed, all in all, I was perfectly happy to be thought cute, whatever label anyone added after that.

When I casually put the harness on the bed, Tess said, "I thought we were going to dinner."

"We are."

"Oh."

"Do you like that idea?"

"Is that why you suggested the dark little place?"

"Yeah."

Tess planted a huge kiss on me. "I really am going to get lucky tonight, aren't I?"

"I'm the lucky one, baby." I kissed her back and it was a long, delicious minute before we resumed dressing for dinner.

"You say the sweetest things," Tess said as she finally let go of me.

"And that's not all." I reached into my suitcase and withdrew the surprise. "Happy anniversary."

"It's not our anniversary—oh wow. That's…wow."

I wiggled the package. Tess was a size queen and I loved finding new ways to make her eyes roll back in her head. "You like?"

"I think I'm going to like, yes." Her tongue darted over her lips and I thought it was highly likely that parts of her had just donned party hats and grabbed the maracas. "How on earth are you going to hide *that* in your pants?"

"Those baggy gangster pants you hate."

"Is that why you brought them? I love those pants now." She was still staring at the toy. "I like that shade of pink too."

"Thought you might."

"It's still not our anniversary."

"Sure it is. We've been together four years, five months and thirteen days."

"I love you." Tess gave the new toy one last fond look. "I'll just go get dressed."

I was glad she disappeared into the bathroom, because

fiddling with the harness and fasteners is really not the sexiest of moments. I finally got Lucky 7—as good a name as any—into the O-ring. It was a pushing, pulling, rolling challenge, and once that was done, I still had to get the harness onto me. I felt silly in the thing at such times. Never silly when I was actually going to get into bed with Tess—I felt alive and needed and incredibly turned on when getting into bed with Tess. But wiggling around and dancing in circles trying to pull up my pants and the toy catching on everything, well it wasn't debonair.

After a one-legged Watusi, I finally had the pants belted around my waist. It really felt weird. I had never worn the thing outside our apartment, but what happens in Vegas stays in Vegas, right? I adjusted the pants on my hips and wriggled until the toy hung down one leg, only losing a few leg hairs in the process. The fabric of the pants wanted to stick to the toy, like silicon had magnetic properties near cotton. Then I realized why it felt weirder than I'd expected. I'd forgotten to put on the boxers. Bold enough to wear the toy outside of the room, but no way was I going without some kind of underwear on—

Tess came out of the bathroom.

Breathe, I told myself.

She was a sensuous vision in a thigh-length aquamarine dress studded with copper beading. The halter neck made her seem even taller.

"I take it from the look on your face that you like this dress?"

I nodded. I had just about found my voice when Tess turned around. Her bare back put me back into the Land of No Breath. The high neck clasped with a twist of beads that dangled along Tess's spine. I wanted to lick my way up her back.

All for you, you incredibly lucky dog.

I watched her put on her favorite sandals. They weren't made for walking, and had, in fact, never been out of our apartment.

She looked up when she'd fastened the last buckle.

"Ready?"

"Uh-huh."

"Don't you think you should put a shirt on?"

"Oh! Crap." I blushed furiously. "That dress is a walking crime."

"I just got it this morning. There was a guy selling dresses out of the back of his van. I only noticed because he had quite a crowd. Twenty bucks. I figured out later he was there to sell stuff to the escort service workers here for that convention." She gave Brandy a worried look. "I don't look like I'm for sale, do I?"

"I will make it plain you're spoken for."

She gave me one of those serious looks that said we would talk about the subject again.

"You don't look cheap or available for the asking, darling." I tucked in my shirt. "You look like the gorgeous, classy creature you are. Not to mention young and attractive."

"You found that gray hair the other day, remember?"

Was that still bothering her? Dunce, I scolded myself. Next time don't point it out. "That was sun streaking."

"If you say so."

"How about this?" I balled my fists on my hips and walked toward Tess like Yul Brynner's King of Siam. "Go out with me, and everyone will know you're mine."

"You look magnificent."

I dropped the attitude. "No, really. Can you see it? Does it show?"

Tess hesitated. "Maybe a little."

So, what was my choice here? Stay in because I was chicken or take the most beautiful woman in the world out for a delicious dinner, get her a little bit tipsy, a lot hot, then bring her back to our room for a night we wouldn't ever forget? Duh. "Nobody is going to be looking at me."

I repeated that to myself all the way to the restaurant. Of course it felt like the entire world was staring at my crotch. The things love made me do... Thankfully, we were quickly seated, which put my crotch out of sight.

After studying the menu and flirting over a glass of wine, we decided to share what turned out to be a wonderful apple and pecan salad, and a perfect steak with Parmesan chips. I enjoyed every moment of watching Tess sparkle in the candlelight. My best friend, my lover—all the beauty in our relationship was on Tess's side of the table, as were most of the brains.

We shared dessert as well, and I found herself a little disappointed. "Your brownies are better than this one."

"It looks like chocolate," Tess said. "But I don't taste it."

"Kind of like cruise ship chocolate. Remember, I told you about the food on the boat?"

"And you told me about nearly being borrowed by that hot butch."

I grinned and shrugged. "She was awfully cute. But I really missed you, and I was thinking about your ankle and how you must be so sorry to be forced to sit at home. I know you wouldn't have minded if she'd borrowed me for a night, but..." I hadn't been able to admit to her that I'd backed out because I'd realized that nobody could touch me, reach into me, the way she did. The okay-to-be-borrowed rule was Tess's, even if neither of us had used it so far.

I didn't want to mess up a really good thing by appearing possessive all of a sudden, but I didn't need the rule.

Tess took my hand, her expression serious again, and I wondered what was bothering her. There was something, but I trusted she would bring it up. She wasn't afraid to talk about anything, and I had already unlearned many bad habits of resentful silence and passive-aggressive fighting that I'd picked up from my dysfunctional, hateful family.

All she said was, "I have a Snickers bar in my suitcase. We could go back to the room for dessert."

"Oh, I'm having dessert in our room, most definitely." For just a moment, I didn't feel awkward as I shifted in my chair suggestively. Tess's quick little exhale was quite gratifying. Apparently, I could pull off the suave, seductive lover thing for a few seconds at a time.

The check paid and our intentions declared, we were back in the faux-fresco painted elevator when a crowd of curvy, slinky, high-heeled, coiffed and elaborately made-up women of all heights and colors crowded on with us.

"I want to dance all night," a bright-eyed Latina said.

"Our own private disco, in the penthouse. I love Vegas."

"Who has the invitation?"

The Latina made eye contact with Tess. "Do I know you from somewhere?"

Tess shrugged. "Probably from around."

"Is that your girlfriend?"

Tess tucked my hand under her arm. "Yep."

"She looks *really* happy to see you."

I could feel a blush spread to the roots of my hair. All the women were giving me the once-over now, gazes lingering south of my waist. "I'm always happy to see her."

"Lucky her," the Latina said. "Maybe I'll get a dance later?"

"We're not—" I realized we'd missed our floor.

The doors opened to a blast of music and the women poured out of the elevator with delighted whoops. The security guard looked helpless as they pushed past him. Caught up in the rush, I found myself jostled along to the parquet dance floor that had been laid out in the suite's living room. It was packed with women, some of whom weren't wearing much. Not that

I minded that part, but I had been hoping to see more of Tess, not a lot of women I didn't know.

"Do you want to stay?"

"Why not?" Tess tucked her little purse down my front pocket. "Dance with me, baby."

It was heaven. We hadn't been on vacation together in so long, and even when we did get to dance on tours and cruises, we were almost always still on the clock—being a tour guide meant there was no "off."

I swayed in Tess's arms, pulling her close, and closer still. Other women were making out as the music pulsed around them, so I felt perfectly natural pulling Tess down to me for the first of a dozen long, luscious kisses.

"You always wind me up," she finally said in my ear. "I'm so torn. I want to dance all night with you, but I also want to…" Her hand moved between us and I shuddered as she gripped the toy through my pants. "What a wonderful dilemma."

"Just because we're getting older and wiser doesn't mean we have to be silly." Ever resourceful, I took her by the hand, leading her away from the dance floor. "If we leave we might not be able to get back in."

I veered past the impromptu bar. Where there was a penthouse there had to be bedrooms. Before Tess, I'd had women in the resort's fitness room storage closet, behind the pool house, once even on the back of a Sea-Doo. Sneaking into a bedroom for a not-so-quickie was positively tame.

"Oh, you are in a mood tonight, aren't you?" She didn't seem the least bit displeased when she figured out what I was thinking.

The first door was locked, the second revealed another couple with the same idea. If they were even aware of the door opening, they didn't show it. A third bedroom was equally occupied, and the bathroom was usable only if one could ignore the noises coming from behind the glass shower doors.

I sighed with frustration.

"Over here," Tess said. She pulled me behind a pair of large potted ficus bushes.

"Baby, anyone can see us."

"Only from the shoulders up. Besides, who here is going to arrest us?"

My pulse reached a boil. "I see your point. So I'll fuck you right here?"

For an answer, she gave me a slack-jawed look and pulled up her dress to reveal that I wasn't the only one who'd gone out without panties.

"Baby." I was stunned. She was in one of her moods, and I loved those moods, but this was more than…beyond even…I might have stood there, mouth hanging open, but fortunately a little voice inside me shouted, "Shut up and fuck her, you idiot!"

I unzipped. "All for you."

"Now," she said, spreading her legs.

It felt like the first time all over again. She made a sound that made my head spin. I pushed harder, paused when Tess reached down. "Is it okay? Damn, we need lube, baby."

"It's fine, just something…there. Oh yes, Brandy, please."

Her hands went down the back of my pants, squeezing and massaging my bare ass. The surge of erotic adrenaline drove every other thought out of my head. I bit her neck, held on, lived all our nights and days over again, felt that electric current of memories that culminated in the promise of a future that went on like this, full of love and passion and play—fucked her through her first climax, knew there would be a second, and relished that knowledge. I loved this woman, loved being with her, and knowing her body the way I did only deepened the magic.

She said my name, gorgeous in her abandon. "Don't stop."

"You know I won't."

"Damn it, Brandy, you know, please…"

Our words danced back and forth, no pattern or reason anyone else would understand, but four years and more of working on our own language meant I knew she wanted hard, deep, steady strokes now, then short ones, softer while she hovered on the edge of climax again. I listened, heard the sharp whimpers. I pinned Tess to the wall, words and little noises all jumbled together.

We drifted in each other's arms on the dance floor. I was zipped and a little bit wobbly in the knees.

"That was incredibly fun."

"It was," I agreed. "Want to do it again?"

"In our room. In just a little while." She ground against me with no rhythm that matched the music, and it was perfect.

A woman paused next to us as we swayed. I recognized the attractive Latina from the elevator. With a direct look at Tess, she said, "Mind if I cut in?"

"As a matter of fact, I do." Tess arched one eyebrow at the woman that plainly said, "Go away."

"Sorry. I know you already got some of what she's packing, and you may have noticed that she's the only one who is. But if you're not sharing, that's cool."

"She's not for borrowing."

The woman shrugged expressively and walked away.

I looked up at Tess, not exactly confused, but I wasn't sure why she had put it quite that way. For a moment, she wouldn't meet my gaze, but then she did with her serious, open expression that I had always found brave and wise. But at the moment it was tinged with chagrin.

"I didn't even ask you if you wanted—"

"I didn't," I assured her. "I *really* didn't and I don't. You're right. I'm not for—"

"I want to make it permanent," she said, all in a rush.

"Are you sure?" My heart melted in my chest.

"No borrowing. No sharing. Just us. I want to be yours." She kissed me softly. "And I want you to be mine."

"Yes." I kissed her back, then nuzzled at the pulse point of her throat.

"I know it'll be the same old, same old, boring and…" Her voice trailed away.

I stepped back to give her an incredulous look. "You're kidding, right? Boring? You?"

She shrugged a big fat it-really-doesn't-bother-me lie and wouldn't look me in the eye.

It was no time to be shy.

"You just let me fuck you in public and we've done a lot of things, but that was the hottest so far, and if you think I'll ever be bored with your body, you're crazy, and right now I want to take you back to our room and do about five hours worth of the same-old-same-old, until we're both sore and exhausted and this new, very lucky toy, is worn down to a nub. Then we're going to start over because the favorite thing I love to hear you say is 'honey, I'm done' and that's what I live for, Tess, that's what I want, you, in my bed because you are every woman all in one, and I love you."

I ran out of breath. She blinked tears out of her eyes. Several women nearby had paused in their dancing, openly smiling.

I ducked my head in embarrassment. When I finally decide to make a speech I really ought to learn to check if I've got an unwanted audience. "Time to go."

She tucked her hand under my arm and nodded.

Once in the elevator, Tess slid her hand down to intertwine our fingers. "Know what?"

I risked a look and found her gazing at me with eyes like stars. "What?"

"I think today really is our anniversary. From now on."

Sugar

Published: 2004
Characters: Sugar Sorenson, cake decorator
               Charlie Bronson, firefighter
Setting: Seattle, Washington

Sixteen candles and no end to the light

The Hardest Part

(3 years)

"Move it! Move IT!" Sugar knew she was screaming, and it was a good thing it was raining. With windows rolled up tight there was little chance of the other drivers hearing her. It felt good to scream. It let off tension, it pushed the fear farther away, right out of the van, somewhere out onto Lake Sammamish.

The wet roads made driving in her usual aggressive style unwise. She curbed her desire to lean on the horn and tried to calm herself. "You're no help to Charlie if you end up in the hospital too."

She'd left Grannie Fulton praying. If anyone had a direct line and could get God or Jesus or some saint to intervene, to make Charlie okay, it was Grannie Fulton. As annoying as the many years of her grandmother's Christian-based homophobia had been, the last few years of loving acceptance, of pleasure at being a family with Sugar and her Charlie, had more than made up for it. Charlie's endless appetite for Grannie's cooking had permanently endeared them to each other. Her crazy schedule as a firefighter didn't interfere with their early start every day, either. Sugar would continue her cake projects while Grannie stirred up the first of many donated desserts and trays of lasagna to the senior center, the halfway house, the women and children's shelter…

Taillights flared red in front of her, reflecting off the wet pavement like fiery jewels. After a moment, the line began to move again. It would be no faster taking surface roads, but the stop-and-go was wearing her nerves to the last degree.

"Please, please," she pleaded with the traffic, but it was more than that. "Please let me get there and it's all a mistake. Please let it be just a scratch. Please…let her be okay."

Captain Johnson had told her not to worry, that it was probably minor. As if *probably* meant anything! She was thankful he had even bothered to call—oh, that wasn't fair. She had no issues with the way the department treated her and Charlie as a couple. Her problem was with the other wives.

The Wives. That's what they called themselves, and that included Tom Perlman, the only male spouse at the stationhouse. Tom took it in good humor. But Sugar heard the little hesitation before the word *wives* when Opal McKay said it. She made sure, every single time, that her referring to all of them as married women was heard as an exceptionally generous gesture on her part because, as everyone knew, Sugar *of course* wasn't married to Charlie.

They weren't *really* a family. But Opal, and her chief toady Heather Wong, allowed them to exist.

She told herself to relax her grip on the steering wheel. It took an effort to unclench her jaw. No, they weren't a real couple, and so Sugar wasn't really a member of the stationhouse family. Not part of the family when everybody else's kids wanted someone to buy wrapping paper or cookie dough or Girl Scout cookies or tickets to a school production. Not part of the family when someone cheerfully accepted her family discount on the latest cake they'd ordered from her.

She was *tolerated*. It stuck in her throat, and anyone who thought a goal in life was to be tolerated hadn't experienced tolerance the way mean-spirited people like Opal McKay could eke it out.

Finally at her exit, she veered off the freeway toward Sacred Heart Hospital, and asked herself what any of that mattered. Charlie's entire unit had been inside a collapsing home, and Captain Johnson had told her—only after she asked—that Charlie hadn't been conscious when the ambulance had taken her away. Alive, but not conscious. He didn't know if there were burns. He didn't really know…how bad it was.

Her cell phone remained silent. She guessed that was a blessing because she couldn't drive and talk and think and not hold back tears of fear and anger. She loved Charlie the firefighter, and loved that Charlie cared so much about saving people and their property, but dear God, she hated the job. She hated *this* about Charlie's job.

She had to circle the hospital twice to find the parking entrance. The rain was pelting down—Seattle, any time of year, night or day, it rained. It wasn't quite six o'clock, but the black clouds hid any sense of a sunset. She put the collar of her jacket up, covered her head with her purse, and ran for the emergency room doors.

The middle-aged woman at the nursing station looked up with a perfunctory smile.

"I'm Charlie Bronson's partner. She's a firefighter, was brought in a while ago. I have her power of attorney, can you tell me how she is?"

107

"The doctor isn't out yet. You can wait with the others. It probably won't be long."

"Can you tell me anything? Was she conscious when she got here? I have a right to know."

With the sigh of someone not unkind but far too busy, the woman tapped at her keyboard. "She wasn't conscious. Suspicion of smoke inhalation, but that was before any further examination. That's all I know."

Dismissed, Sugar turned away, but she wanted to demand to be taken to Charlie, scream the place down until someone let her see Charlie's face.

The Wives were all there, in the waiting area. She didn't know if they'd seen her. She didn't care. She went the other direction and found a chair as far away as she could. She had no sooner sat down than the adrenaline that had gotten her here shut off. Her legs and arms were shaking and she couldn't stop the tears of worry.

She fished a tissue out of her purse, but it was quickly soaked. She didn't have another, and didn't have the strength to fetch a paper towel from the restroom. She sat there, her face covered with tears, clutching her purse over her stomach.

"Here, honey," someone said.

She fumbled for the offered tissue, then accepted a second one. "Thank you."

"The waiting's the hardest part."

She glanced up and was surprised to find Opal McKay gazing down at her. The usually carefully constructed makeup was absent and her eyes were rimmed in red.

"Come over with us, honey. It helps not to be alone."

"I don't think I can," Sugar managed to say. Her voice sounded like old corn meal on cold marble.

Opal misunderstood her. "I'll give you an arm to lean on. It'll be okay, honey."

Don't call me honey, Sugar wanted to yell. She couldn't find the voice for it, nor a voice to say she couldn't handle being tolerated right then.

She shook her head.

"I've been here too many times not to know that it'll help to be together."

Sugar didn't know quite how Opal managed it, but she was making her unsteady way across the room, leaning heavily on Opal for support. "It's just reaction. I'm okay."

"Oh, we all know," Opal said. "It takes everything you have to get here without running someone off the road. Then you feel like they should be checking you in too. It'll ease in a bit."

They made room for her, Heather moving a little more slowly than the rest. Four frightened women and one frightened man with an austere captain trying to look resigned and hopeful all at once—they were a silent bunch. Every other minute someone would briefly share whatever news they'd been told, as if it had changed, as if they hadn't told it before.

Maha Pashmir got up to pace. "Three minutes, and then I'm going to make a scene. We should have had an update by now."

Tom Perlman said mildly, "I'd rather the doctor dealt with Judith than calming me down."

"The doctor is done by now," Maha said. "We're waiting on some factotum to deliver us a message." Her voice rose.

"Maybe someone should ask," Heather said, giving Captain Johnson a glance before turning a falsely sweet smile on Sugar. "I'm sure the captain can get information for you too."

Sugar shook so hard with anger that her vision of Heather's smug little mouth broke into little pieces.

"Enough of that," Opal snapped. "Nobody in this hospital is going to treat Sugar any different."

"No." Sugar's lips were so tight she could hardly form the words. "No, treating me like I don't matter is what you all get to do."

There was a sharp, strained silence. I probably shouldn't have said that, Sugar thought. *But what the hell does their good opinion matter right now?*

Heather was looking daggers at her, but said nothing.

"I deserve that," Opal said finally. "Stupid thing, something like that has to happen before I see sense." She cleared her throat. "When you came in I felt like Jesus was whispering in my ear that I knew full well what the right thing to do was. You were suffering just like we are, and no little piece of paper makes a bit of difference. Your Charlie, my Ron—"

Her voice broke, and the last few hours only became more surreal because Sugar sat in the emergency room, holding Opal McKay's hand.

She would never understand why it was so hard for people to see that love mattered, most of all.

"The waiting's the hardest part," she murmured to Opal.

"It is, honey. It really is."

Heather's shocked expression and Maha's continued pacing distracted Sugar from the arrival of a tall woman in green scrubs.

"I'm Dr. Watson, and I was the lead on the team that worked on your people. I'll make a group announcement, since the report is all the same. There was serious smoke inhalation, but all the oxygen levels are on their way back to normal. We want them here for another couple of hours so we can take another blood sample and monitor lung function. Give us a few minutes and you can each go on back. They're all in the same exam area."

As they gave the doctor a chorus of "Thank yous," Captain Johnson, who had been stoically silent and stalwart the whole while, abruptly sat down.

"The waiting's the hardest part," Opal said to him.

Heather and Maha were murmuring thanks to different deities and Sugar flipped open her phone to call Grannie

Fulton.

"My grandmother was worried," she explained to Opal after the exchange of a few heartening sentences with her grandmother. "She adores Charlie more than she likes me, I think. She's going to let my sisters know the news."

"How many sisters do you have?"

"Three. They treat me like a baby, but they call it love."

"I'm the youngest of five."

Just like that, they were chatting, and the worry drained out through the soles of Sugar's feet. She felt a little bit numb. And how exactly was she supposed to go forward, all forgiven, with Opal? And Heather? Charlie put up with it because she had the undying fraternal support of her fellow firefighters all the rest of the year. But they'd made life really unpleasant for Sugar the last few years—been mean and cold at birthday parties, pointedly and precisely correct at Judith Perlman's father's funeral with not one fake smile to spare, even stiff and withdrawn at the annual picnics where everyone ended up smeared in watermelon. The whispered fuss they'd made about making sure their kids didn't accidentally have any of the food she and Charlie brought—turning their noses up at Grannie's lasagna, for heaven's sake! But they all had Sugar's cake, slicing up the fire engine after admiring how realistic it was.

What would Grannie Fulton do? She thought it over until a nurse came to tell them they could go in to the back.

When she stood up she said to Opal, "Thank you."

It was a start.

Charlie's creased and ash-smeared face was a welcome sight. Sugar thought her heart would burst from relief.

"You're a sight," she said, brushing at the ash with her

fingertips. Heedless of any of the other wives, she gave Charlie's smiling lips a quick kiss.

"Do you know if the kid is okay?" Charlie's hoarse question was underscored by a worry, deep in her eyes.

"What kid? We don't know anything. I suppose Captain Johnson knows."

"He wasn't there." Charlie squeezed her hand. "I'm so glad you're here. Wanted you to hear the doctor. I'm fine."

"You don't look it." Sugar traced the line of the IV drip from the back of Charlie's hand to a pouch hanging next to the bed.

"I just need a shower."

"You need a rest." Sugar gave her another kiss before straightening up. "Behave or Grannie Fulton will hear of it." As her own heart rate finally calmed she was aware that the room reeked of wet, burnt wood. The hospital was going to need a lot of Febreze when they were released.

Charlie pulled a face of mock horror before saying, "There was a kid—house fire. Got away from his folks and ran in for the cat. We had all taken off our masks, and mine was mostly secure but there was no time—kid didn't know the roof was done. I thought it was Hopkins who got him."

"He went in the other ambulance, probably to Puget Medical." Judith Perlman spoke up from the next examination table. "I was out of it pretty much—didn't see if the kid was with him."

"Maybe the captain can find out." Sugar recognized Ray McKay's deep voice. "Do something useful for once."

There was laughter until the Captain quelled them with a loudly cleared throat. "If you're done having your fun, the child is fine. He'll have some burns to show off. And the rest of your team is at Puget Medical, lounging around just like you lot. Nobody knows anything about the cat."

The squad burst into laughter again, and when Captain

112

Johnson tried to get their attention, and failed, he pronounced them all high on oxygen, which brought on another wave of hooting.

"You're going to pull out your IV," Sugar warned.

Ray McKay tried to sit up and Opal pushed him right back down. "Enough of that. Not until the doctor says."

"Aw, honey, I don't need a doctor to tell me when I'm fine. Chuck," he called. "Talk some sense into them."

Sugar turned her head in time to see Charlie's father, Chuck, take in the scene and visibly relax. He strolled toward Charlie's bed. "Not on your life. I have a heart condition, remember?"

His glance at Sugar was anything but nonchalant. He was a retired firefighter, and had probably left home moments after Grannie Fulton's first call. She answered his question with her eyes, then followed his shifting gaze to Charlie's face.

There was definitely more pink in her lips now. The skin that Sugar so loved to rest her cheek against, that was a perfect match to her favorite mocha-chocolate cake icing, was less waxen.

Nevertheless, Chuck leaned over his daughter and said, "You look like hell. Do what Sugar tells you."

Without hesitation, Charlie said, "This from the world's worst patient—and there are nurses in this very hospital who will attest to that."

Sugar loved the way Charlie's eyes flooded with affection for her father. Such wonderful expressive eyes.

"Oh go turn those puppy dog eyes on someone else," Chuck said.

She found herself enveloped in the melting, brown gaze. "Nope," Sugar said, though her voice didn't have quite the conviction she'd hoped for. "Not going to work on me either. You are going to do exactly what the doctor says. And another thing," she added, her voice rising. "I would really appreciate it if you tried harder not to scare the living crap out of me again."

Too late she realized that a silence had fallen, and everyone in the room heard her remarks, loud and clear. She felt a blush start in her cheeks, but Opal smacked her husband lightly on the shoulder.

"What Sugar said. You put me through too much."

"Yeah," Maha and Tom echoed. Even Heather made some sound of agreement.

Suddenly, they were all in the same pose, arms crossed firmly over their chests, and Sugar finally felt like one of The Wives.

She caught Opal watching her and Charlie with Chuck, then their gazes met. If hers held a plea, she wasn't aware of it, but Opal gave a little nod. Yes, Sugar thought, this really is what it's all about.

A nurse came in to check all the monitors, and the firefighters went back to ribbing Captain Johnson. Sugar wanted to take Charlie home, tuck her in bed and feed her Gran's chicken soup for the next year. But it wasn't time yet, and waiting was the hardest part.

Touchwood

Published:	1990
Characters:	Rayann Germaine, wood sculptor and advertising artist
	Louisa Thatcher, bookstore owner
Setting:	Oakland, California

The Second is for Spilling Over

The Curve of Her

(3 years)

I am watching her at the top of the sliding ladder, her weight all on one foot while she uses the other as a counter-balance to the arm that stretches for a book almost out of reach. She is a curve of hip, a sweep of hair, then a flash of humor as she hands the volume down to the waiting customer.

"That do it for you today, Belle?" I take the hefty Hemingway anthology from her to put in a bag.

"Thanks, Louisa." Belle pats her pockets in search of her credit cards. "I don't know why Jean likes Hemingway, but it's her birthday tomorrow and she doesn't have this collection yet."

"Girlfriends," I joke. "Can't live with 'em, can't live without 'em."

"Hey," Rayann protests from the top of the ladder, where she is spreading books out on the shelf to hide the large gap where the anthology had been. I watch her fingers on the spines of the volumes, savoring the texture in the same way that I do. I think, then, of her fingers on my skin.

I'm intensely aware of Rayann shimmying down the ladder. The fog of the past week has finally given way to summer heat, at least here in our part of Oakland, and forced her into a simple top and shorts, with the skimpiest of sandals passing for footwear. Her figure seems more ripe and alluring at thirty-two than it was at twenty-nine. She complains about the effects of gravity but I always tell her she hasn't seen anything yet. When she's my age—just shy of fifty-nine—gravity will be an old friend.

She disappears into the recesses of the store. During our vacation, an enthusiastic volunteer made a mess of shelving the new paperbacks and Rayann has been steadily putting things right. I wave goodbye to Belle and go in search of her. I need to gaze at her today; I want more than that.

She is frowning and muttering to herself as she kneels in front of the lower shelves, but the frown dissolves when she looks up at me. "Maybe when we go away we should just tell them not to…"

My silence is heavy with desire, then after a moment, her response twines into that silent wanting and I see her arms prickle with gooseflesh.

The silence is broken by her whispered, "Lou," and then she lifts her face. Standing over her I cup my hands in her hair, loving the curving line from her chin to her throat to her breasts. I kiss her then because her eyes ask me to.

When our mouths part she murmurs, "After last night—"

"Because of last night," I answer, after I have kissed her again.

She pulls me down to her and I am—perpetually—in awe

of her love for me. I never thought I would have this mystery again. I loved Chris as much and as deeply. When she died in that car crash I thought that was all the love there was for me, and for a long time it had been enough. Years later, Rayann burst into my life, then into my bed.

There is never any danger of mistaking Rayann for Chris—Chris would never have pulled my hands to her breasts, not in the daylight, nor with the lights on, not in the back of the store, no matter how much she wanted me.

Rayann and I were wild together last night and this passion is all the more surprising because of that. She is shivering at the threshold of surrender. Only the time and place holds her back. The bell at the door could ring at any moment, but when she wants me this way, when I want her this way, it will be impossible to stop once I have touched her.

She is unzipping her shorts, inviting my hand inside. Chris—the only other lover I have ever had—would never have done that. There were so many things Chris and I never did, even in our most private moments, things Rayann takes for granted. She grew up in a different world, never having been closeted. Chris and I lived in two closets, the first to hide who we were from employers and my son's teachers, and the second for the benefit of friends we could not and did not want to survive without.

Rayann still does not understand. I've told her how many times how my best friend Danny was arrested for not having enough items of women's clothing on her, how anyone who suspected I was a lesbian could make a call to social welfare to send someone prying into my suitability as a mother. But part of her can't understand and in a way I'm glad of that. Her innocence gives her the freedom to want me like this, to be panting in my arms, to surrender so readily, without worrying if society or friends would approve of who does what, of who goes first, of who comes and how.

I was a mother, and mothers weren't butches. Danny impressed that rule upon me forty years ago. In the world I navigated then, it made sense. Never mind that the labels Danny and our other friends insisted on were backward for me and Chris. Friendship and staunch loyalty meant more to me—and to Chris as well—than any concession I might make over a simple label. We needed our friends and never questioned that we had to hide a part of ourselves to keep them. We were living together, and happy. Back then it was nearly an impossible dream. But it is also true that it was only when we were truly alone, in the dark, that we were free to be who we really were.

Chris would shiver the same way Rayann does, but at this moment, in the dark, Chris would have whispered, "Please make love to me."

In broad daylight, a product of a different world, Rayann pushes my hand down her hip and moans urgently, "Fuck me."

It makes me dizzy that she has forgotten where we are. For a moment I think the ringing in my ears is faintness but it's the door. A customer. She is too shattered to move, so I get up, kissing the blushing angles of her face one last time.

The afternoon drags on and I catch Rayann watching me as I am watching her, aware of what we want, knowing we will wait, and feeling every tick of the clock as a pulse of building desire. Fifteen minutes before closing she announces that she's going upstairs to our apartment. She'll make a light dinner. I tell her I'll close up.

Only ten minutes have elapsed when the door opens and Danny comes in, her swagger, leather jacket and thick denims a familiar and loved sight. But tonight I'm hoping she's just stopped in to pick up a book for Marilyn. No such luck—she pours herself the last cup of coffee and settles in for a chat.

I go through the motions of closing up and like every other time she has dropped by near closing time, she follows me into the stairwell and locks the door behind us, then tromps right behind me up to the door to the apartment. I open the door and can only say, "Uh…"

Danny gasps, then grins. She hits me on the shoulder. "I'm in the way, aren't I?" She steps delicately over the trail of clothing Rayann has left, pointing the way to our bedroom.

Rayann, clad only in a very short silk robe that I bought her as an anniversary gift, says, "Oh my God," and disappears from the bedroom doorway.

"I'll just let myself out," Danny says, heading for the apartment's back door, not one whit embarrassed. "You have a nice evening, now. Come to think of it, I have a lady at home who might need taking care of too."

The door slams and Rayann peeks out the bedroom door. "I'm sorry," she begins.

I am across the room in moments, seizing her by the shoulders, kissing her hard, then pulling her breathlessly to the nearby kitchen table. I am dying for her and she cries out when I take her, her hand circling my wrist as my fingers dive into her heat.

She clings to me with another cry, her legs circling my hips. She makes my head spin. I can't believe she can yield so quickly, and with such strength. She gives and takes in a moment like this, and doing both—letting me know with her body, her voice—only makes me want to please her even more. My own trembling begins. She opens new doors in me, doors that Chris never knew existed. Doors I have deliberately ignored.

Her head is on my shoulder. The first storm has passed. I am listening to her gasp and loving the sound of it when I hear a voice.

"You might want to close the windows," Danny calls smugly from the street in front of the house.

"Oh my God," Rayann says again. She is blushing as she hides her face in my hair. She can't see that I am blushing too.

My stomach is flip-flopping as I close the windows while she goes into the bedroom to do the same there. She is sitting in the shadows of the tapestry over our bed when I join her, her mouth looking swollen. I abruptly understand why I'm thinking about Chris and Danny and labels. I had thought my mind was over it. My body seems to be. Tonight, with her looking at me like that, I am wanting her touch. If I was over these labels, my stomach wouldn't be churning.

I want to give myself to her. Nearly six decades and still I can see myself anew.

I draw the curtains against the evening sun, wanting the dim light because I am on unfamiliar ground.

She undresses me eagerly, her mouth on my throat, my breasts. Until tonight I have thought of this as indulging her need for foreplay; she knows I am usually satisfied when she is.

I am cresting on a river of fluid self-perception, too old not to understand that anything, anyone can change, and still young enough to revel in new experience. With Chris, always in the dark, she wanted me inside her. I loved to inhale her female scent, to taste it until her hands were in my hair, holding me there. I found my own climax—when I needed it—on top of her, straddling her thigh as she touched me. Rayann knows this and has never asked me to be different for her. But tonight, deep in the well of her forthright desire, I am changing anyway. Chris would never have wanted what Rayann needs at this moment, and for the first time in my life I need it too.

She looks up at me, her eyes full of hunger, her lips curved in thirst. I love filling my mouth with her, knowing her in the most intimate way. She wants to feel that powerful intimacy and I don't want to withhold it from her just because of a label.

I'm not indulging her. Finally, I am aware that I can give and take at the same moment. I want her mouth on me, now. I want it so badly my legs won't support me. She is on top of me and I cannot believe the sensation of her skin on mine. I have seen burning fires in her eyes when she calls my name, but I am the one in flames tonight. My temples are pounding and I make a sound—a plea, an order, something in between.

Her mouth engulfs me. I am washed over with a wave of pleasure that leaves every muscle taut, anticipating. I feel the tensing of her shoulders under my thighs. I have loved giving her what she wants and this is no different. She wants me to come. I never have like this, but I can't help it, I don't want to help it. My satisfaction is hers. The battle between past and present is academic. I am opening, offering, clenching, shaking. Her muted cry answers my release. I give her what she wants and finally see that it only makes me stronger.

I manage to raise myself onto my elbows, so I can look at her as she pants for breath after her mouth leaves me. My God, but I love her. I stretch to stroke her cheek and her eyes flutter open. The desire in them is even brighter than before. Partly because I love her so, but mostly because I want it, I cup the back of her head and draw her to me again. Her moan sends a shiver through my hips. Words finally escape me. "Ray, I didn't know."

I don't know if she hears me. It doesn't matter. I think of Chris, who let me be this to her. I remember the first time I was with Rayann, who let me be this to her. She devotes herself to my pleasure with her tongue, her teeth, then one slender finger is inside me and I go with the new wave of ecstasy, spreading from her hands and mouth and into parts of me that have never ached before.

I am impossibly drained. For the first time in my life I consider dozing off before my partner does.

Rayann murmurs, "Thank you," as I often do when I have exhausted her. I hear the pleasure in her voice.

"I'm not done with you," I tell her, though my eyes are closed. "I'm just savoring how wonderful that was."

"Have a nap," she whispers.

"Tempting, but I want you too much to sleep."

She says something, almost shyly, but it's lost in my hair as she turns her head away.

"What did you say?" My fingers at her chin, I turn her face toward me.

She sends a jolt through my spine with, "Prove it."

Car Pool

Published: 1992
Characters: Anthea Rossignole, cost accountant
               Shay Sumoto, environmental engineer
               Adrian and Harold, gay male friends
Setting: Oakland to San Jose, California, and along
               highways, side streets and bridges in between

The Fourth is for Freedom

Divided Highway

(18 years)

"It's the next left." Anthea watched Shay's hands on the steering wheel, but today the usually welcome sight was just a blur. Her eyes wouldn't stay focused.

"I'll come in with you." Shay's voice had the same raw edge that Anthea's did, a painful combination of shed and unshed tears.

"That's probably not a good idea. Twice the lesbians isn't going to make this any easier."

"Yeah. I mean, what am I? Just the other mother."

She put her hand on Shay's thigh, knowing the bitterness wasn't directed at her. They'd all like to direct their anger toward something useful instead of doctors and laboratories and tiny type on computer printouts.

Shay navigated the worn Oakland neighborhood street, pausing for children playing and avoiding potholes and the occasionally oddly parked car. Anthea wondered which of these houses was the one where Harold had grown up. They'd passed his school a few blocks over, and he'd said there used to be roses along the front—but he hadn't been back since the last disastrous conversation with his mother eight years ago. He'd hoped the prospect of a grandchild where she'd had no hope of one might soften her poisonous homophobia. But she was having none of his evil plan to make a baby with one of his lesbian friends and raise that baby as part of a four-parent household. The child that Anthea had carried to term had never known his father's mother.

Beautiful Henry, with his father's melting eyes and winsome ways, knew Adrian's parents well. They'd been elated to have a surprise grandchild and hadn't expected Adrian to ever be a father. They didn't care in the least that their son's husband was the biological father, and that Henry spent half his life with his biological mother, Anthea, and her wife Shay. Lots of kids had two moms and two dads, after all, though most perhaps not in that combination, and in the Bay Area biracial kids were less and less rare. They all lived within a few miles of each other in the wooded Oakland hills, and Henry never wanted for a parent's or grandparent's attention. He had thrived—until six months ago when unexplained weight loss had led to blood work and finally to this narrow street.

Beautiful Henry—Anthea turned her head so Shay wouldn't see her lower lip quiver. Just when she thought she was all cried out fresh tears would threaten. She knew she cried mostly from tension, but Shay saw the tears as despair. None of them had cried until this week, after Henry's first chemo round and the news that Harold and she, his closest biological ties, had not tested very highly as bone marrow donors. Shay and Adrian's results were—not unsurprisingly—

even less promising. The national registry of people willing to donate bone marrow hadn't found a strong match either. Henry was home now with Adrian, finally able to enjoy food, but the next round was tomorrow.

In the meantime, the doctor had told them to find family members to be tested as matches "just in case." The idea that Henry could suffer so much with no benefit from it had left Anthea numb. But she didn't despair, not while there was a chance that Harold's mother and cousins who had similarly cut him off might possibly test as better bone marrow donors than Harold.

"I think this is it. Do you think she'll be home?" Shay drifted to a stop at the curb in front of a neatly maintained bungalow.

Anthea glanced at the dashboard clock. "Harold said she preferred the early shift, so if nothing's changed, she got home from work about an hour ago. Hopefully has had time to eat some lunch." She blinked at the blue sky—the sun was blazing overhead. She supposed it was unseasonably warm for Oakland in June, but none of the heat seemed to penetrate her. "If nothing else I'll camp here until she shows up. What other choice do we have?"

Shay's short laugh had no humor. "I thought I knew all about pride. March, yell, dare the bullies. All the things you're willing to do. All the things you believe you'd never do because you're out and proud. Never ask a favor from a homophobe. Live without them. Never show weakness or deny who you are." Her fingers clenched around Anthea's. "But what does anyone know about pride if they've never had a sick child?"

Anthea didn't dare look at her. They'd both be crying if she did. She held Shay's hand until Shay let go to get a tissue from the box between their seats.

"I sat with my dad, all those months." Shay wiped her nose. "I was helpless and angry, watching him slowly waste to nothing. I hated cigarettes—I knew what was killing him. But…it wasn't like this. Nothing to blame. And what point is pride when it comes to Henry? Whatever that mean old woman wants she can have. Anything. Anything if it'll save Henry."

Anthea had to clear her throat before she could speak. "Would you sleep with Mel Gibson?"

"Oh that's so gross." Shay sniffed.

Anthea patted her hand. Before their viability test results came back, Shay would have laughed at the poor attempt at a joke.

She peered at the bungalow's tidy yard. Roses, a vibrant showing of pink, salmon and cherry red, filled the beds that flanked the front door. She clutched the file folder to her chest. She didn't know what she was going to say. But Shay was right. She'd say anything, promise anything—there was no point to principles and pride. She'd join the Westboro Baptist Church if it would save Henry.

"Here goes nothing."

"Good luck, honey. Goddess and Wicca and rainbow flags and the Force and Xena and all things bright and beautiful— may they be on our side."

"There's just one side," she said. "Henry's."

"I'll be right here."

Heart pounding, certain of a disdainful and angry reception, she resolutely made her way up the short walk to the front door.

She had never met Harold's mother, but seen pictures many times when she and Shay had dined at Harold and Adrian's. Over the years the photographs had no doubt gone out of date, but the woman who answered her ring of the doorbell looked much like the woman on Harold's wall. With the light flowing from behind Anthea, she could see Mrs. Johnson easily through the screen door. Her hair was pure white and close cropped to her dark, regal, beautifully-shaped head—an attractive feature that Harold and Henry had both inherited. Her frame was angular and lean. Her dark face was heavily lined—prayer had not brought her peace, that was for sure.

"Can I help you?"

Anthea was momentarily thrown by the fact that her voice was husky, like Harold's. Reminding herself that Mrs. Johnson had raised a fine man who respected women and life, she said carefully, "I'm Anthea Rossignole, Henry's mother."

After the briefest of pauses, Mrs. Johnson asked, "Why are you here?"

It was that tiny hesitation that gave her a small ray of hope. Mrs. Johnson knew something was amiss, and cared to find out if her son was okay. "Henry needs your help. Only you can give it."

"I was very clear with Harold. I don't approve and I can't have anything to do—"

"Henry has leukemia."

If ever a word stopped a conversation, it was that one. The lines around the older woman's eyes deepened.

Anthea had dealt with a lot of executives who refused to understand the absolute nature of a balance sheet's bottom line. Many of them, when shown that their company would not be able to make the next day's payroll, flinched. They turned their heads, looked at the door and then they retrenched to their position of denial. She saw Mrs. Johnson head begin to shake *no*, and her shoulders twitched as if she would shut the door and keep the unpleasant news on the outside.

Stepping to one side as if expecting the screen door to be opened for her, Anthea asked, "May I come in, ma'am?"

Whether it was shock or simply good manners was of no matter to Anthea. The screen door opened and she was inside. A few moments later the front door closed behind them and the outside world winked out of existence for her—Anthea could no longer remember if it was sunny or foggy, summer or winter. She did remember the aching, terrifying moment that she had told Shay she loved her. She had thought then that nothing she would ever say could possibly be more important.

"Would you like some coffee?" The offer was perfunctory.

"Only if you have it made, ma'am. Otherwise, a glass of water would be perfect."

"I do have some made fresh. I was just home from work a while ago."

"That would be wonderful, then. Just black coffee is fine."

She perched on the edge of the indicated stiff-backed chair and raised her voice slightly so it would carry to the kitchen, just visible through the doorway on the other side of the living room. "Harold said you might be home by now."

"Did he send you?"

"No. But he knows I'm here. He thought if he came it would upset you more."

Mrs. Johnson reappeared with a delicate tea cup and saucer. "I won't change my mind. The church is very clear. I love my son but I hate his sin."

Anthea accepted the coffee, pausing to admire the rose and heather china pattern. At least she hoped Mrs. Johnson thought that's what she was doing. There was no place in this room for her anger. Instead, she recalled their stalwart, dearly departed Mrs. Giordano, whose staunch Catholic faith had given her the strength to face down her priest several times about the church's stance on homosexuality. "They're God's children, same as you and me," she had recounted telling him more than once. "And maybe a bit more, because he picked them for a harder journey right from the start."

"I'm not here to talk about sin. I'm here to talk about a child." Anthea sipped the coffee, tasted nothing, but smiled anyway. "It's delicious. Thank you."

She set the tea cup in its saucer on the delicate side table, then opened the file folder on her lap. "Your grandson Henry is sick. We're trying to find a match strong enough to be a reliable donor—"

"If I understood my son correctly, he was reliable enough, when you wanted him to be."

She was so nonplussed by Mrs. Johnson's direct reference to the way Henry had been conceived that she blinked. She hadn't expected Harold's mother to go *there*. "He was because we all wanted one thing." She held up an 8-by-10 of Henry.

Any hope she had that the picture would be enough was dashed by the arched eyebrow. "He's a lovely boy, just like his father. But as I told Harold, my conscience will not allow me to be drawn into a family situation of which I so completely disapprove."

She nearly made the mistake of taking the casual way the words were delivered as a sign of detachment. It was the tiny tremor of Mrs. Johnson's tea cup that slowed her response. Every word she said mattered, and she realized she was talking to a very angry woman.

"We would welcome you into our family, and Henry would love to have another grandparent, but that's not why I'm here. None of us match as bone marrow donors, not well enough. It would be very risky, desperate to try. But you could be a better match. Harold also thought you might know how he could contact his cousins. One of them may also be a good match. Henry is undergoing chemotherapy now." She swallowed hard.

Holding up the photo again, she added, "He's lost about twenty pounds since this was taken. We think the chemotherapy will work. But if it doesn't we need to have marrow donors lined up. We will need to act quickly. He's a child, barely eight, and so things don't always go as planned."

"No." She shook her head. "I'm sorry you've wasted your time, but no. My conscience won't let me. It's not easy, it's never easy, but God gave me faith strong enough to conquer temptations of the heart."

Anthea reminded herself that the reason Harold didn't know his father was because Mrs. Johnson didn't know the name of the man who had assaulted her. Her marriage, when Harold was still a toddler, had been short-lived. She had not had an easy life, but, Anthea also reminded herself, that was no excuse for taking it out on a child. "Harold is a good father. He is loving and kind, but firm."

"Patronizing me won't work, Miss Rossig…"

"Rossignole. It's French for nightingale." She sipped the coffee again, as if they were just two ladies sharing polite conversation. "Your son is a fine man."

"A real man marries a woman."

She had to set the cup down or it was going to snap in her hand. "He takes responsibility for his life, for his own actions. He left the refinery, and works with my wife doing environmental studies. Sumoto and Johnson—they're in demand these days. He cares about the planet. He cares about his son." He's not the man who raped you, Anthea wanted to say. He's a better kind of man, the way you raised him to be.

"This changes nothing. If I was going to change my mind, I would have done it years ago. Do you think I don't want to be a grandmama? But I can't."

"You're missing so much."

The older woman turned her gaze to the simple cross that hung over the small fireplace. "My road isn't easy. Don't think I do this because it's easy."

"I think you do it only because it's hard." She hadn't meant to say that, but the words bubbled out. "Just because love is easy doesn't mean it's wrong. It's *supposed* to be easy when it comes to children. That's how God made us. He's only a boy and he's already been through so much. We can lose him altogether—but you have the power to give us hope."

"If there's hope, God will give it to you. It doesn't come from me."

"Why not *through* you, from him?"

"That's not his plan."

She couldn't keep her voice from shaking. "It sounds to me like it's not his plan, it's *your* plan. The chaplin at the hospital and Harold's husband's rabbi, they both told me the same thing. That even though it's hard and I may not understand it, this is God's plan for Henry."

Mrs. Johnson nodded. "It's not for us to question or understand. He gives us our path and we must walk it."

"So I'm supposed to fight it, struggle against it, but take comfort that if I lose, it's okay, I lost to God? God did what was best?"

With a hint of suspicion Mrs. Johnson confirmed, "Of course, child. But I can have no debate with you that I haven't had with myself. The Bible condemns—and before you say it also condemns many other things that are commonplace, like wearing mixed fabrics and working on Sundays, I'm not talking about your Bible. My Bible says the way you live your life is a sin."

So much for the idea that she could fake agreeing with Mrs. Johnson in any way. "What about the Episcopalians and Quakers? The Unitarians and even the Lutherans?"

"Their Bible is fine for them. I live by mine." Her answer bordered on smug. "I was baptized by its guidance, and saved throughout my life by its light. It truly lifts me up from dark places."

If she'd known Mrs. Johnson had already studied up on the debate, she would have done more homework. Leviticus was riddled with inconsistencies and rules that nobody followed—including animal sacrifice—so she'd been primed to point out that the Bible's application to life evolved. She had hoped to find at least one piece of common ground.

"It lifts you up, but I am in my darkest place." Anthea cleared her throat. "And it's your Bible, not mine, that will keep me there. And none of this has anything to do with Henry. His sickness may be part of God's plan, but then so is the reality that you have a choice. Maybe Henry is sick to make you realize what you're choosing—words on a page or the life of a child."

"They're not just words on a page." The smugness was gone, and only an implacable, cold rage was left. For someone who thought she had all the answers, Mrs. Johnson didn't appear to be completely sanguine about God's plan for her.

"Isn't Harold part of God's plan? Isn't having a gay son part of God's plan for you? A plan that brought you a grandson? Whatever sin you may see in Harold, and me, it's not Henry's sin. But I am part of God's design, Mrs. Johnson. Outside in a car is the woman that I love, and God designed me to love her."

"God made you. The devil brought the temptation."

"She isn't a temptation—she is a salvation. For me. Not for you, but for me. And it still has nothing to do with Henry."

Mrs. Johnson rose abruptly, but Anthea didn't follow suit.

"Harold is a fine man, loving and honest. Strong, such a good father. You raised him to be good all the way through."

She looked down at Anthea. "He took everything I gave him and made it dirty. I won't have anything to do with any of this."

"I'll come back." Anthea tried her best not to sound mulish. "Until you change your mind."

"My mind won't change."

"Being a good Christian is not an excuse to be cruel. I know my Bible, Mrs. Johnson, and Jesus did not like cruelty. Love God, and love thy neighbor. If your own grandson isn't your neighbor, then who is? You'd cross the street to help a stranger in pain, but not your own blood? Is that really what

Jesus died for?"

"I'd like you to go now."

Aching with misery, Anthea stood up, leaving the photograph of Henry on the coffee table.

As she left, she noted the cross next to the door, like some kind of sigil to ward off evil. She fumbled in her purse for a tissue and tried to stifle her tears, but her heart was breaking, just the way it had every day of the last week. They all loved Henry so much, and love wasn't enough. It didn't warm this hateful woman's heart, and it wouldn't stop the tears.

"Thank you for the coffee," she managed before the door closed behind her. It was hard to see the steps through her tears, but she made it down them without falling, even though her knees threatened to buckle.

Shay met her halfway up the walk, her eyes shimmering with matching tears. "As bad as Harold said?"

Anthea could only nod. Shay's arms were around her and they had never been so welcome. "I don't know what we're going to do."

"Hire a private detective to find the cousins. It won't take very long to do it. Surely one of them has a decent heart."

Anthea reached the car. "Let's get out of here. I made such a mess of it."

"Miss Rossig…Rossignole."

Surprised, and her heart suddenly pounding, Anthea turned around.

Mrs. Johnson was making her way down the few steps, looking as if her hips hurt with the effort. Anthea walked toward her and took a proffered paper from her hand.

"That's Harold's eldest cousin. He may help. He went to seminary, though. I don't know if he will."

"Perhaps he'll be a truly godly man, then." It stuck in her throat, but she said, "Thank you."

"Would you—I would like to know what happens." Her

eyes were focused on some point over Anthea's head.

She found a business card, turned it over and wrote her cell phone number and email, then quickly added Harold's as well. "You only have to call or write."

It was all she was going to give in return for the phone number. If Mrs. Johnson wanted to know her grandson's fate, she would have to earn that knowledge by making contact. Maybe she was the one being a little cruel, and not entirely Christian, but she was flawed, and had never claimed to be a good anything—except a good wife and a good mother. The rest could wait.

They had turned the corner at the top of the street before Anthea said, "I want a shower."

"I'll bet." Shay took her hand.

"Harold is amazing. He survived life with that woman."

"She was probably a good mother until he came out. And you know, call me an optimist, but I think she'll write."

"I really don't care," Anthea said. "I don't care about her soul or Christianity and the politics of reconciliation."

Shay squeezed her fingers. "There's only Henry. The doctors said his odds with chemo were really good. This may not matter in the end."

"But it's the only thing we can do." She smoothed the paper with the hastily written name and phone number. It was a local area code. "Another call to make."

"More chemo tomorrow."

She closed her eyes and focused on the warmth of Shay's palm against hers. No matter where this road ended, Shay was her one, solid ground.

Paperback Romance

Published: 1991
Characters: Carolyn Vincense, romance novelist
               Alison McNamara, Carolyn's agent
Setting: Hot spots of Europe and Sacramento,
               California

The Third is for Turning On

Payout

(19 years)

"So how does it feel in the light of morning?" Alison spooned behind Carolyn, massaging her shoulders gently as the sun slowly illuminated their hotel room. It amazed her that it was so quiet when only a few floors away the cacophony of an enormous tourist mecca with thousands of conventioneers was so deafening it made her head ache every time they crossed it to get to the romance writer's conference.

"I'm still not sure." Carolyn rolled onto her stomach. "Your hands are wonderful, as always."

Alison shifted her position, continuing the soft touches with one lazy hand. "I know you're young for this sort of thing, but then you started out young as a published writer too."

"True. I just…" Carolyn stretched out an arm to touch the

Lucite statue of an old-fashioned oil lamp that rested on the bedside table. "It's an award, and it's been a long time since I've seen one."

There was the tiniest edge of bitterness in Carolyn's voice, and it pained Alison. "You wouldn't do it any other way, would you?"

"Of course not." She snuggled around in Alison's arms. "I'm glad I came out. I'm glad I've been living free. I just feel a little bit young to get the Lamplight Award."

"You did light the way, and it was very cool that Amelia Wainwright was the one who presented it to you, and I swear, Barrett Lancey had tears in her butch little eyes. They wouldn't be who they are if Carly Vincent, hot new best seller, sweetheart of the twenty-four to thirty-two demographic, hadn't taken one for the Sappho team dang near twenty years ago. Other romance writers could have come out, no doubt, but you're the one that did it."

"I was waiting on the world to change and it did, I guess. I didn't lose all my readers."

"Just the narrow-minded ones, and you weren't writing for them anyway. I'm glad you don't regret it."

"I don't." The eyes that gazed up at Alison were still the clear blue she'd lost her heart to. "I might whine a little sometimes, but I don't regret it. I've loved the life that being out let me live. With you."

"God, you feel good this morning." Alison breathed in the cologne, the shampoo, the wonderful blend of scents that equaled Carolyn to her. "I loved dancing with you last night. I can't imagine living a life where I didn't get to dance with you in public."

"Me too." Carolyn burrowed into Alison's shoulder.

"It was a fun evening, even if Farrah Fotheringay was hitting on you." Romance writers were such interesting creatures. As an agent, Alison had never ceased to be intrigued by their eccentricities. Not that she thought it was eccentric to be attracted to her Carolyn.

"Was not. She's straight. She probably just wants a new agent."

"No, she was after the hottest woman in the room."

Carolyn twisted a lock of Alison's hair around her finger. "I love the way your hair is changing color, silver and platinum threads all woven in."

Alison smoothed her love's short curls and turned the adorable face up so she could see it. All these years and it was still like waking up to sunshine. Sleepy eyes blinked at her. "I love you."

"You're just saying that." Carolyn stretched.

"Why would I just make it up after all this time?"

"Because you want to have your way with me."

Alison cupped one alluring breast under the covers. It firmed at her touch. "I don't know what you're talking about."

"It was late last night, and I recall being promised something if I wore those thigh-high stockings that get you all hot and bothered. But alas, all I remember were some vague mumbles about wine and the hour." Carolyn's light tone was at odds with the small arch of her back in response to the tip of Alison's finger lightly stroking under her nipple.

"Then I need to make it up to you, don't I?"

"I would think so."

"Okay." Alison threw back the covers and hopped out of bed. "How about a nice breakfast?"

"Get back in this bed this instant." Carolyn gave her a wry look.

"Oh, so you want breakfast in bed."

Carolyn dissolved into laughter. "Honey, I want to *be* breakfast in bed."

"My thought exactly."

She began with slow kisses along Carolyn's calves, eliciting a soft, encouraging sigh. She would never get enough of the taste of Carolyn's skin, and lazily worked her way up the welcoming, curvaceous body. It made sense to get out of her nightshirt then, and use her breasts to massage Carolyn's thighs.

A long, rising moan rewarded her efforts and Alison stretched out so their bodies could meet in the full delight of skin-on-skin.

"Ally," Carolyn breathed. "You've got some kind of magic hands."

"Tell that to my teammates. I drop any more fly balls and—"

Carolyn pressed her fingertips to Alison's mouth. "Why on earth are you talking about softball at this moment?"

"Cause mostly...I'm an idiot?"

The little laugh they shared was intimate and ended with the kind of kiss that reminded Alison of the backseat of Carolyn's old Mustang convertible. Now was not the time to admit she was having a fast food craving. Other cravings took precedence.

"Close your eyes," Alison whispered. "Think about Melissa and the concert tonight and the backstage passes your fabulous agent got you."

Carolyn laughed again. "I thought they were a birthday gift from my girlfriend."

Alison kissed away the laughter—she loved doing that. She loved making her Carrie laugh and then moan ever so slightly. Every time they shared this dance it had all the fever and fireworks of their first time, combined with layers of familiarity. There was still plenty of mystery, but no terror of doing something wrong or too hard or too soft. Make her laugh, and kiss the smiles.

She could do this all morning.

She did do it all morning, as it turned out. No doubt Carolyn would have the right metaphor for the way her body was melting over the bed, spreading like warm honey, only not so sticky and leaving a less romantic soul to wonder who was going to clean all that up.

"More, Ally, please…"

Those were Alison's favorite words.

Her second favorite set of words were said shortly thereafter.

"Your turn." Carolyn gave her a searing look, no longer melted honey or melted anything, she was firm and soft all at once, just a little commanding and more than a little eager.

Alison moaned when Carolyn's tongue found her most tingling places, then she couldn't help but laugh.

Carolyn immediately stopped what she was doing. "Am I distracting you?"

"Sorry, honey. I was just—I realized how good it was to moan really loudly and not have one of the puppies come to investigate what we're doing."

Carolyn grinned and kissed Alison's inner thigh. "Okay, yes, that is nice. But no more laughing." Her tongue pressed into the soft place where thigh met really sensitive areas.

"Hell, no, oh…"

She scrabbled among the rumpled sheets for Carolyn's hand as her legs fell open and she lost herself in the exquisite attentions of that wonderful, thorough mouth. She felt the love all through her bones, and she did want to smile at her happiness. Another laugh threatened— maybe it was watching her beloved Carrie, who had suffered in classy silence all these years after the onslaught of hate mail and plummeting sales, publicly recognized by her peers as the brave woman she was. It had been a risk, and there had been a price, but now—

Carolyn's sensitive fingers moved inside her and the

laughter transformed to passion. Her memories of last night, dancing, her daily ecstasy of waking up with Carolyn, they went away and the only focus she had was for the pressure building behind her eyes, along her shoulders, down her arms to where her hand clasped Carolyn's. She rose, Carolyn held on, their bodies frozen until a white, hazy afterglow gently surrounded her.

"Did I go to sleep?"

Carolyn leaned against the bathroom door, drying her hair. "Yes. And you missed the chance to shower with me."

"Damn." Alison stretched, not wanting to get out of the bed.

"Honey, there are two floors of casinos, five swimming pools, three hundred fountains, and an art gallery waiting for us, now that the convention is over."

"Um-hmm." Carolyn's mouth had felt wonderful, she mused.

The bed jolted from Carolyn's swift kick. "So get up!"

Alison reluctantly swung her legs over the side of the bed. "If only your fans knew what Carly Vincent is really like." Her gaze fell on the award and she touched it with one fingertip.

Crossing the warm carpet to the bathroom, she turned Carolyn from the mirror to take her into her arms. "You know, right? That I'm proud of you, that you're the world to me? That I love you?"

"I know." Her smile was soft and easy, completely unshadowed. "I was feeling sorry for myself last night, for a while. But this morning, today—I know why I made those choices. I got everything that ever had value to me. I got you."

"Let's go back to bed."

"You just want to sleep more."

"We can play breakfast in bed again, first." She blinked innocently.

Carolyn laughed and Alison kissed the smile.

In Every Port

Published: 1989
Characters: Jessica Brian, management consultant
               Cat Merrill, hotel management executive
Setting: San Francisco, California, 1978

The First is for Filling Up

Filled to Overflowing

(32 years)

"I think I've got a blister, but that hike was worth every step. This has been the vacation of a lifetime." Cat leaned into Jessica and closed her eyes.

Jessica slipped an arm around her beloved as the little passenger sea shuttle bounced over waves on the way back to the massive cruise ship. "We actually stood on Lesbos. I'm blown away."

Truthfully, Jessica's feet were throbbing too, but a soak in the ship's hot tub before the promised pastry extravaganza at dinner would make it all better. Some sips of that nice ruby port Herine had given them as a bon voyage gift would also be dandy.

Cat stirred against her. "I wonder how Kitty is doing

with—"

"Nuh-uh." She shook a warning finger at Cat. "We are not grandmothers this week. Therefore do not mention the grandchildren. We agreed."

"I know. It's hard not to wonder, though." Cat straightened up, her gaze fixed on the rapidly looming ship. Wind from the open windows of the shuttle boat lifted her hair from her shoulders. Jessica loved the soft golden color—in the not too distant future it would probably be snowy white, far more attractive than the faded black her own hair had become.

"Every day for the last three years, nearly, we've been part of their lives. It's only right that Rob's parents get this week. I'm sure everyone is doing well." She resolutely did not voice any of the many petty thoughts she'd had at the idea that Kitty and Billy might call someone else Meemaw.

Cat squeezed her hand sympathetically. "We were on Lesbos."

She squinted as a shaft of sunlight lanced off the brilliant white hull as their shuttle slowed on approach. "I was just thinking about that bottle of port Herine gave us."

Cat made a little purring noise. "Now that sounds heavenly. She's a good kid—picked up your discerning taste in the finer things in life."

"You're on that list, you know."

"A finer thing in life?" Cat gave her a narrow look. "I'm not sure I like sharing a list with a nice brie or oak-and-cherry notes in port."

One of their fellow passengers laughed. "She has you now, mate."

Jessica grinned back. "From the moment we met."

The other woman gave her own partner a squeeze. "We're celebrating our fifteenth."

"Thirty-two—our daughter and her husband bought us the tickets."

She and Cat murmured thanks to the chorus of congratulations. Recognition was welcome, but it also underscored that she and Cat were considerably older than most of the other passengers.

Their little shuttle tied up at the docking plank. She made sure Cat safely navigated the steps and then accepted the hand of the crew member to gain solid footing on the deck. It was a mild day, but it still seemed as if the deck was pitching madly.

"I can't wait to get out of these shoes," Cat said.

"Let's get right into our swimsuits," she suggested.

"Now you're talking."

A half-hour later they shared sips from a paper cup after they'd eased their sore bodies into the hot tub on the main pool deck. Dinner service had begun so it wasn't as full of people as usual. Jessica closed her eyes and let the bubbles at her feet soothe her.

"We were on Lesbos," Cat said again.

In her mind's eye Jessica could picture the time-worn temple and other landmarks of the island's history. Though there was nothing overtly welcoming to lesbian pilgrims, she had no trouble envisioning acolytes in gossamer gowns carrying laurel-scented water to wash the feet of the poetess.

Her reverie was interrupted by the noisy arrival of two young women she recalled from the tour. They plopped in the water and sighed with relief.

"I'm whacked," one said.

"Totally. I'm still disappointed, though. All that dust and ruin and that's what we're all called? Because somebody wrote some poems?"

Her companion shrugged. "Poetry is dead."

Jessica gave Cat a sidelong glance and then looked away with a deep breath.

"Actually…" Cat paused to casually sip again from the paper cup. "Poetry's immortality is what allowed our foremothers to adapt the island's name to describe a society of women for women. Had Sappho's verse not survived there's no telling what we'd be calling ourselves, and we might still be searching for a collective identity that allows us to bond and struggle for the advancement of our rights. Without the word *lesbian* we'd not be on this cruise, or it would be called something else."

The two women were looking at Cat as if she were speaking Greek, which might not be far from the truth. Jessica wiggled her toes in the bubbles and watched her beloved through her lashes.

Cat smiled brightly. "If you think about it, the words we use to describe our gender describe not what we are, but what we are not. Fe*male*. Wo*man*. Not male, not man. In contrast, *lesbian* is an assertive word that states what we are in relation to ourselves and no other construct. Sappho's work that survives, and that of her contemporaries, indicates that her academy was likely only for women. Certainly, in our modern age, we want to romanticize this as an act of feminist rebellion when she was a member of a family persecuted into exile. She chose to eschew the influence of men thereafter, probably because it was one of them that brought the wrath of the rulers down on her. Societies run by women *had* nearly disappeared by Sappho's time. We look back at her academy and see it as a continuation of the line of matriarchy. A bright moment in the long, dark fall of women from their place of respect as givers of life."

The poor young things were deer caught in Cat's headlights. That they were ignorant of women's history wasn't their fault—they obviously hadn't had Cat for a mother.

"I expected something more," one of them muttered. "That's all I meant. Everybody goes on and on about her poetry."

"So little has survived, it's true. But it has inspired our lives. *For while I gazed, in transport tossed, my breath was gone, my voice was lost, my bosom glowed*—"

"Sounds like she'd had a very good time at some point," Jessica said drolly.

Cat splashed her with water. "Hush, you."

The other young thing cocked her head to one side. "That sounds familiar. The voice lost and bosom glowed part."

"Those lines were used in one of the songs Marcy Chastain did Sunday night. She obviously found them inspirational."

"Cool. Lyrics that are three thousand years old—I wouldn't have guessed."

"Marcy's so hot," the other said with a sigh.

They slipped into conversation between them the two of them after that, and Jessica stole a glance at Cat, who was basking in the hot water while a satisfied smile played around her lips. Leaning over, she said, "I'm going to tell Herine you used her honor's thesis to scold two baby dykes in the hot tub."

Cat snorted. "Think they want to hear about how much dead poetry is in the song lyrics they enjoy every day?"

Given that the two girls were now making out, Jessica shook her head. "They have a few good ideas, though."

Cat gave her an amused glance. "I'm all relaxed now. What about you?"

Jessica drained the last of the port. "I'm dandy."

Cat was stripping off her swimsuit in their stateroom as the light from the porthole cast blue shadows over her shoulders. Jessica sidled up behind her to nuzzle her neck.

"Wanna be a little late to dinner?"

"Is that what you have in mind?" Cat wrapped Jessica's arms around her waist. Thirty-plus years and they still fit together exceedingly well.

"Port...warmth...thoughts of licentious acolytes and

glowing bosoms."

"And you an old lady."

"Dirty old lady."

Cat turned in her arms and lifted her mouth. "Thank goodness, because I'm one too."

The days of romping across the bed in abandon had been over from the moment Jessica had first slipped a disk, and other delights were curtailed because Cat's knees protested forty-five degree or sharper angles. They'd adapted, however, to all the limitations age was putting on them. Sensible crones, as Cat called them, made use of modern science.

They slid between the cool, dry sheets on the double bed as Jessica retrieved the slender bottle of personal lubricant from the bedside table. "I love this stuff. Fountain of youth for the lady parts."

Cat grinned. "So do I. When I'm in the mood I do like to be wet."

"And when you're wet..." Jessica gently spread the lube over Cat with sure fingers. "You're in the mood."

"I should insure your hands."

Jessica kissed the lips curved in a fond smile, then pressed more firmly with her fingertips. Cat's response was quite gratifying. A few whispered words and they were moving together, sweet and easy, not forcing the tide, but letting it rise to wash over them. The motion of the ship lulled them into a soft pace, and kisses were long and languid until they were panting more than kissing.

"Touching you like this is my very favorite thing," Jessica whispered.

Cat's shivers were so familiar to Jessica. "I'm so glad, because if it wasn't you should have said so before this."

She pulled Jessica down for a wet, deep kiss and delightful muscles gripped at Jessica's fingers until Cat gasped for breath and made that wonderful sound. Jessica went in a little deeper, drawing out every bit of response she could.

Cat relaxed and laughed. "God, that's fun."

"Well, if it wasn't you should have said so before this."

"Foo."

"Is that the best you can do? Got no brains at the moment?"

"Foo."

"There's supposed to be chocolate at dinner."

Cat abruptly wiggled and pushed until Jessica found herself on her back. "We'll get there, but there's something else I'd rather eat first."

Jessica grinned. "Do you have a reservation?"

Cat quickly slipped her hips between Jessica's thighs, then deftly tickled the sensitive patch along her underarm. While Jessica struggled and laughed, she continued her downward journey until the laughter faded and there was only the intimate exploration of Cat's tongue where Jessica never tired of feeling it. Today would be one of those times when she didn't climax, but the soothing, relaxing pleasure of Cat's attention left her feeling a glow that would last for hours. It was a different kind of sex for her and as meaningful to her at this age as other kinds had been when she was younger.

There was a moment she reached when it felt as if Cat had filled her to overflowing and she could take no more. It didn't matter that certain muscles no longer experienced spasms as easily, not when she reveled in the heat of Cat's mouth, feeling the wonder of it in all the places only Cat had ever reached. She laughed, low, and stopped Cat with a soft gesture. They smiled over the length of Jessica's body. "Better than a hot tub."

Two beautifully arched eyebrows disappeared under Cat's bangs. "I should hope so."

"Come here, you." Jessica opened her arms and they snuggled together under the covers.

"We smell a bit funky now."

"I like it."

Cat's breathing quickly steadied and Jessica decided another ten minutes wouldn't matter to whatever was served for dinner. Cat was warm and safe in her arms. Someone else might think that they'd sleep together later, so why give up a unique experience in favor of one she could have almost any time she wanted?

Then again, some people didn't get it.

Substitute for Love

Published: 2001
Characters: Holly Markham, mathematician
               Reyna Putnam, public relations
Setting: Orange County, California

Twelve Flowers were Their Gift to Say...

Reconciliation

(10 years)

"I think it's letting up." Holly moved the windshield wiper knob down one setting and the *slap-thunk* rhythm slowed. Somewhere, and years ago in all likelihood, an engineer had decided that given the variables of the wiper length, motor speed and windshield slope and size, that this speed of steady swipes would efficiently clear water during the most common volume of "light rain." That, or the engineer had simply copied the last engineer's decisions. Life was full of shortcuts. Sometimes they made no significant difference. Sometimes they meant that neither setting one or two was the right choice for basic precipitation.

Drops on the hood of the rental car pooled and separated in a chaotic dance. She wasn't surprised that Reyna hadn't answered her comment. There was a lot on Reyna's mind, none of it particularly pleasant.

"I read another blog about the big coming out." She and Reyna had been spiritedly debating the politics of a highly placed GOP strategist announcing he was gay and switching all of his gay-related politics 180 degrees. "This one insisted that his participation in creating the Defense of Marriage Act was costing gays and lesbians and their allies millions and millions of dollars in legal fees and lost benefits, and that no mere fundraiser was ever going to even the scales. That there was no way he could ever make up the lost time to the legal spouses from other countries who couldn't come to the US because their US and/or European marriages and right to immigrate were denied by the federal government."

It was at least something to talk about. Better than the reason for the rental car and the grim hours that lay ahead of them. She shifted the speed of the wipers up for a couple of swipes, then turned it down again. She was willing to bet the settings were copied from those for a larger car—they were definitely off. She'd driven a hundred rental cars in the last ten years and this was at the bottom of the list for weather controls, unable to handle a typical rainy November morning in Los Angeles.

Reyna suddenly said, "Right side."

"Oh, sorry." Holly guided the car back into the right-hand lane of the access road. Spending most of the year at Oxford made readjusting to U.S. driving difficult. "So if the blogger is right, you and I being treated as single when we're married according to the state of Iowa, is a financial burden that this guy caused us."

Reyna continued to gaze out her window. "Nobody has that much power. No one person can influence that many lives. It takes willing accomplices."

Glad to finally be pointed the right direction on the

405, she merged out to the fast lane and kept up with traffic, remembering the way with ease. With customs and LAX finally behind them, their first destination was the Putnam Institute, the conservative think tank foundation that Reyna's father had founded. Holly thought the demand for a meeting uncivilized, given the circumstances, but Reyna had consented. She would listen. I didn't mean she'd agree to anything. She was, after all, a Putnam.

"They might as well blame me for Proposition 8," Reyna continued. "They were still flogging the talking points I developed for my father on the evils of gay marriage." She sighed. "If this guy has half a soul, he feels like crap, and he's going to take crap for years. And he should. I did."

If anyone was going to sympathize with the newly out pariah it would be Reyna. Her circumstances were different, though. Few people knew that Reyna's complicity with her father's ultra-conservative agenda had been compelled by a very personal form of blackmail. There had been some comment—short-lived—when Reyna had not appeared with her father at the inauguration that had made him Vice president. But to some she would always be the bastard child, an indiscretion, so not for the bright, pure light of great ceremony.

Ill-health was the only reason Grip Putnam hadn't run for the Oval Office at the end of his eight-year VP stint. He might have won, Holly mused, even though he was a symbol of the deep economic mess the eight years had created. Ironic that his heart gave him trouble when a lot of people didn't think he had one. To this day, Holly heard Darth Vader music in her head whenever she thought of him.

Finally in smoother traffic, Holly reached for Reyna's hand. "It might as well be London," she said, meaning the rain.

"I could seriously go for a steak and stilton with a Jameson's." Reyna lifted Holly's hand to hold between both of hers. "You didn't exactly get a bargain with me, did you? All this…angst. The calls Thursday didn't stop. Reporters don't care about time differences and you in the middle of exams."

"Stop that."

It had been a long time since Reyna had been so depressed about her unhappy past, but then they more or less lived in England and she hadn't had to deal with much about her father in spite of his political prominence. Grip Putnam's daughter being an out lesbian was gossip-worthy, but being married to a professor of mathematics—one who taught at Oxford and was known to lapse into mathematic idioms during interviews—took the shine off the story.

"I got you," Holly said, "and I was meant to be with you. I am the luckiest woman in the world."

"You," Reyna said with a hint of a smile, "don't believe in luck. There is no such thing as luck, I've been told. By you."

"The kind of luck that led me to you is simply an experience we've not yet been able to express in an equation. I am content to call the yet-to-be discovered equation by the name 'luck.'"

"Full of it, that's you."

Holly was so happy to see the teasing grin that she felt herself finally relax. It was going to be a beast of a day. At least she could make Reyna smile. She fished in the backpack she'd slung onto the floor behind Reyna's seat for the not quite finished bag of plain M&Ms. "Chocolate pills?"

Reyna shook out a few, then emptied the rest of the bag onto Holly's palm. "We can at least get In-N-Out burgers while we're here."

"Our dollars to a conservative-owned company?" Holly's stomach growled—it knew no politics.

"I am just guessing that we're funding less evil with two burgers than we are with the tank of gas we'll have to buy sooner or later."

Feeling better for the little bits of candy, Holly said, "Point taken. Burgers are the one thing I really miss about American cooking. Well, from a restaurant."

"I'm glad we're having dinner with Audra. I'll need her mac and cheese by then."

"She texted that it's all ready for the oven, plus that marvelous frozen pea and crab salad she makes."

Finally, Reyna's smile wasn't strained. "Okay, that sounds simply delicious. I can get through whatever hell they throw my way."

"Of course you can, darling." Holly gave Reyna's fingers a last squeeze before returning both hands to the wheel. It was time to negotiate off-ramps and boulevards. "If they think differently they're the fools. The math says odds are on you."

"In a fair fight."

"You still have your mother's memoir notes, and they can still tarnish your father's image."

"They don't have quite the punch they did a week ago."

"True," Holly had to admit. "But while the room might be filled with Grip Putnam's influence and ego, his body is shortly to be six feet under."

Reyna didn't answer right away and Holly worried she'd been too blunt. She couldn't hide her lack of regret that the great Grip Putnam had finally met his maker. She cherished a vision of Jesus with a report card and a big red pen saying, "I gave you two rules, just two! How did you fail the assignment so completely?"

Finally, Reyna said, "I still don't know how I feel. I knew him so well, and I hated him so much. He did right by my mother, finally. Her last year was bearable and she died peacefully… And in his very strange way, he still loved her."

"*Strange* covers it. He didn't love the way you and I do—the way most people can. But I know it's hard on you."

Reyna nodded and the former gloom returned to the car.

The solidity of Holly was like a balm. From the day they'd met, Holly had brought a certainty to Reyna that life contained love, and it was unquestioning, stalwart, honest and palpable. Holly also meant that she deserved that kind of love, though sometimes she wondered what she had done to earn it.

Not today. She didn't wonder today. As they pulled into the nearly deserted parking lot of the Putnam Institute's main building, she felt instead the familiar loathing. Her father had always controlled her upbringing by giving and withholding money, but after his wife and son had died in an accident, his scrutiny of her life had become intense. He'd bartered her mother's medical bills for Reyna's life and energy. She had given up lovers, a social life and her own conscience to the breaking point. And then Holly had crashed into her life. Holly had blown down the house of cards that had preserved Reyna's sanity. Shattered by love, she'd found a way to rebuild her life. Her mother's memoir notes had given her freedom from her father's iron hold—blackmail ran in the family.

Holly managed the umbrella as they made their way to the main doors. Reyna recognized the guard who let them in and nodded. His quiet, "My condolences, Miss Putnam," made her stop and thank him. His tone was human and honest— and very likely the only measure of those qualities she'd find within these walls. When the doors shushed closed behind her she felt a shiver of dread and was glad of Holly's quiet step next to hers as they crossed the cold, echoing marble.

She had decided to wear the suit she had bought for her TED University lecture. She considered that lecture the height of her career as a speaker on rhetoric and political communications. The all-black light wool with a blazer that nodded toward an aviator's cut gave her confidence. It reminded her of the nights she'd ridden for hours, just the

166

bike and the road, and a long way from the misery of her days. She hadn't thought she'd care much about what she wore today, but she supposed she was her father's daughter. He had never appeared anywhere without a careful decision about his appearance. She just wanted the photographers and commentators to have nothing to say so they would all go away. She had done the talk show circuit and had no desire to return to the scream-anything-to-keep-the-camera-on-you tactics.

They were met at the elevators by a bland-faced factotum of some sort. Young, no doubt zealous in his work, he greeted them politely, gave her perfunctory condolences for which she thanked him in kind. He pressed the button for the top floor—it looked like they were going to be dragged all the way to the executive board room. She knew who was waiting and as they walked down the long hallway to the imposing double doors she felt the hair on the back of her neck bristle. If she were a cat she'd have entered the walnut-paneled room hissing.

"Reyna, my dear, thank you for coming on this sad day." Before Reyna could evade him, Danforth Jackson Hobson IV had seized her hand and given it a shake, calculated to the last degree to be both warm and bracing. But his eyes still burned with a zealot's fire and Reyna had no trouble envisioning him in some previous life with a torch ready to light a witch's pyre.

Her skin crawled as she extricated her hand. "It is a sad day."

Hobson hesitated before likewise shaking Holly's hand.

"My wife, Dr. Holly Markham," Reyna said.

In the past ten years, Hobson had learned to school his reactions better. There was almost no sign of his discomfiture at having to nod and acknowledge Holly's full status in the midst of introductions, but Reyna caught him glancing at his hand after he'd let go of Holly's as if he wanted a sanitary wipe.

Only when Hobson had stepped back—which told Reyna all she needed to know about who had called this meeting and who had the highest stakes in an outcome—did the other members of the board come forward. She greeted the five men by name and made them all greet Holly. One big happy family.

The last person she greeted was Paul Johnson, her father's personal assistant. Of everyone in the room he looked the worst—his eyes were rimmed with red and Reyna could not recall ever seeing him less than flawlessly turned out. But today his suit was slightly crumpled and his tie tack didn't match his cuff links.

It was entirely possible that he was grieving the most of anyone in her father's life. She had loathed his hypocrisy for a long time. A supposed ex-gay man, who had married and become a father after undergoing the "treatment" ministry offered by Hobson's followers, Paul had been the poster child for reparative therapy. She had come to pity him, after catching him in an unguarded look he had directed at her father. Sublimating love and lust with work left scars, and she knew that road. She abruptly wanted to comfort him, to tell him she understood that the closet had this price—the love he'd kept hidden for a decade and the suffering he felt now would never know acknowledgement. But that didn't make them any less real. She caught herself before saying anything untoward—Paul had made his own bed.

"Shall we sit down?" Hobson was all congeniality.

Holly didn't move toward the conference table and Reyna realized she had already counted the chairs. They were one short.

"We, ah, we'd like to keep this meeting to members of the board." Hobson smiled benignly as his gaze drifted briefly to Holly.

"But I'm not a member of the board...yet," Reyna said. "On today of all days, I want my wife with me." She gestured at Paul. Maybe that wasn't fair. Long-conditioned, he immediately rose and fetched a chair from the corner, inserting it so that Holly could sit next to Reyna. It earned him a look of contempt from Hobson, but he didn't see it.

They had all settled into the supple leather seats before Reyna continued, "I don't understand why we are meeting now, before the funeral and before the reading of the will. Are you telling me that he left no other directive than his will?"

"He rescinded his nomination directive," Paul said, then he gulped back to silence at a glare from Hobson.

"Indeed, we have no formal notification of your father's nominee for his seat as chairman of our board." The other vice chairman, Seth Miller and Dobson's equal on paper only, was someone she had never known well when she'd worked for her father. A gifted researcher, she recalled, but not gifted in communications. "We assume it's in his will, therefore."

"Why do you think he nominated me? We haven't spoken in any depth in years."

No immediate answer seemed forthcoming. Reyna had always liked Holly's axiom: solve for the simplest solution. That they were even having this meeting meant Hobson wasn't sure it was him. He wanted to lay some groundwork if it wasn't. To make it clear who really ran things even if he continued as the board's vice chairman instead of the new chairman. "Then what's our purpose here, right now, before the funeral and having any information we'd need to make a plan for going forward?"

"If you are your father's nominee, what do you intend to do?" Hobson had that paternal smile that said he'd pat her on the head if she gave the right answer.

"I haven't given it any thought, and I won't unless I have to." Reyna nearly rose, having said all she intended to say.

"You live in England most of the year."

"That's where my wife's work is. She's with the Mathematical Institute of the University of Oxford." Suck on it, Reyna thought. Go ahead, call us elitist because my wife is brilliant and you can't solve for X. Great, she was already resorting to mental sarcasm, which meant it really was time to leave.

"From that distance, it's not clear that you would have sufficient contact to function as chairman of our board."

"You don't have WiFi?"

Seth Miller smothered a laugh as Hobson's normally pale face reddened. Well, it was good to know that Hobson was ruling a divided roost.

Holly suddenly rose. "I'm sorry, but I really must ask where the bathroom is. Sorry, Reyna. I'll be right back."

"I'll show you where it is," Paul said.

Nothing changed with the two of them gone. Reyna smiled blandly at Hobson's various talking points on how she would really not like being chairman of the Putnam Institute. She knew she wouldn't like it. She knew she wouldn't do it. But if her father had left her his seat—she knew the Bylaws, it was his to give—she would have to figure out how to dispose of it. Right now, all her thoughts centered around screwing Danforth Jackson Hobson IV as much as possible in the process. Childish? Yes. But nowhere was it written she had to be grown up all the time.

"Thank you," Holly said to Paul. "I should have asked our escort to stop. It was a long drive and the endless supply of soda on the flight has caught up with me."

"I'll wait right here," Paul said, after pointing out the door. Obviously, she was not being given rein to wander the building. Whatever, she just wanted to use the facilities and wash her hands. Not wanting to abandon Reyna for too long she was quick about it and rejoined Paul in the hallway in short order.

"Ms. Markham, I was wondering if you would give Ms. Putnam a message from me. I can't deliver it directly."

"I will do my best." Holly noted that his steps had slowed. She was pretty sure he was the assistant that Reyna said had been in love with her father for years.

"Mr. Putnam and Mr. Dobson had had a big falling out—it happened over a year ago, as soon as Mr. Putnam returned to his duties full time here, after we left Washington. Though he… In order to support the campaign he had to eschew… I mean to say that—"

"He had to pander to Dobson and his hateful followers to get elected."

Paul swallowed. "It wasn't something he did easily and he didn't like that those people had no sense of compromise."

"Fascists don't compromise—sorry, I'm interrupting." Holly thought there was little to be gained by preaching to this choir. "So you would like me to tell my wife that information?"

"If you would. I know that his will authorizes releasing his letter of nomination for his seat. She shouldn't say or do anything until it's read. But he hasn't nominated her. When he made his decision we discussed it at length. Mr. Dobson is going to be very unhappy."

"You?"

"Heavens no! I'm hardly qualified!" Paul, who had been studying his feet, finally met her gaze. "Mr. Miller."

Holly didn't want to admit that she didn't keep up on the various people involved in the Putnam Institute. Miller was one of the men in the meeting, but she was clueless about his politics. As when a student sometimes talked over her head—it happened—she nodded wisely. "He's more…measured in his feelings on this issue, then?"

Paul nodded vigorously. "Mr. Miller is all about finding out where the gulf is between what people think and the goals of the Institute, so that we can address their concerns and create an effective message. Mr. Dobson ignores the data. Public opinion *has* changed. And I know Mr. Miller's appointment means finally a permanent shift in the Institute's focus as Mr. Putnam wanted. He never had the time to make it happen when he was in office, of course. Then when we got back home he was wasn't well. And now..." His voice broke.

Not knowing much about him it seemed like the only thing to do to put her hand on his arm and give it a sympathetic squeeze. "This must be hard on you."

The look she got said she had no idea, no true idea, of how difficult it was. Reyna had said he was tortured. So sad...not just to ignore who you are but pretend to be exactly what you aren't.

He resumed walking, more briskly, toward the board room. "This is my business card. My private number is on the back. If after the reading of the will she wants more information she can call me. Please don't—please only tell her we had this conversation."

"Of course. Your secret is safe with me."

She meant the note, but he stumbled slightly and looked panic stricken.

"That one too," she added.

"I'm not... There's..."

"Your heart and soul are not my concern, Paul." Though older than her by a few years, he reminded her of a student penitent coming to her for absolution over an academic misdeed. "I'm not judging you. You've given that power to others."

The atmosphere in the board room was as tense as a math department meeting with office space at stake. Reyna had laser beams for eyes and that hateful Hobson man looked like he had spit up in his mouth.

"Glad you're back, darling. We really should go." Reyna stood and turned her attention back to the room. "Other people have stolen your thunder, gentlemen. The newsertainers are getting rich not selling your vision of faith, morality and God, but fear. Any kind of fear, including fear of *you*. If you can produce studies and papers that make people afraid, you're of use to them. If you don't, you're part of the progressive conspiracy or a Nazi, take your pick. You gave those non-thinking loud mouths unlimited power because you thought they worked for you. They took your trust and looted our national treasury, wasted billions and billions of dollars in foreign wars and they have perfected being able to look someone in the face and say tax cuts for them and no health care for you is patriotic. You reap what you sow—now where have I heard that before?"

She turned to Holly. "We have a funeral to get to."

"Yes, we do." And we're walking away from one now, Holly thought.

No one followed them, though the rumble of voices was audible the moment the door was closed.

"That was sort of both barrels, wasn't it?"

"They're irrelevant, but they don't know it. I don't know what I'm going to do if he left me that bloody position."

"He didn't." She recounted her conversation with Paul and handed her the business card once they were in the car.

"Seth Miller, well, he's not a bad choice. He's not so much a policy wonk as he is a data wonk. Let the data speak for itself. Well, I'm glad I won't be mired in it. It's not good for me." She held out shaking hands. "I think my blood pressure was off the charts."

"Well, there's just a funeral to get through now."

"I know. And the press. The reading of the will tomorrow.

I don't know if he'll have left me any money, but I can think of lots of ways to get rid of it that he would simply loathe and I would love—and that my mother would have loved."

Holly focused her eyes on the road, but she reached over to rest her hand on Reyna's thigh. The gulf between father and daughter was enormous, Holly thought, and Grip Putnam's position was now final. She thought of Paul and the gulf between him and a life of freedom. His choices were complicated by a wife and children, and the pressure from people like Dobson to "be a man" was endless, regardless of the damage it caused.

If she made the gulf between the two sides the equal sign, and each side of the gulf the equation that must match the other, then what variables could adjust the constants so that the equal sign became a bridge? So many students derided the philosophy requirements in their math degree curriculum, but she loved looking at social problems that way—and it gave her distance, which was sometimes useful.

The difficulty was that as long as hate was a constant for people like Hobson, she didn't see how the sides could ever reconcile. Well…time would solve that. Eventually, the Hobsons of the world died. Perhaps they would all be better off making sure he had no heirs to his kingdom of hate. She had hope in her students, who cared far more about her power over their marks than they did who she was sleeping with.

The rental car wipers were still inadequate, but the rain seemed to finally be letting up. As they approached the Irvine community center she clasped Reyna's hand. "One of the variables in this is the power you give it to worry you."

"I know," Reyna said softly. "This is temporary. It is the last of him. He did his best to take you away, but I won. I have you. I have our life. *We* are not a variable."

One Degree of Separation

Published: 2003
Characters: Marian Pardoo, librarian
                Liddy Peel, researcher
Setting: Iowa City, Iowa

Fourteen and Fortunately no longer a Felony

Twenty-One

(5 years)

"Swear to freakin' god, look at this place!" Liddy did a little dance as she ogled the big roulette wheel, the recessed area where poker tables were lined up like green jewels and the gleaming rows of clanging slot machines. Over there they were playing baccarat, craps, *everything*. "Kid. Candy store. Me!"

Marian laughed and gave her an indulgent look. "I'll go to my workshop—remember? Work-related conference that's paying our hotel bill? You play the tables. But stick within your budget, okay?"

"I know." She gave Marian her most innocent look. "I can stretch a dollar a long, long way." She glanced around—they were a long way from the openness of Iowa City. They were surrounded by librarians, though, who were a mostly liberal lot. She seized her courage and gave Marian a resounding smooch, then bounded away to the change machine.

Video poker was her first stop.

Twenty minutes and twenty dollars later, she thought if she wanted to just throw her money away, she could play keno. Buy an Edge or Top-Bottom ticket and kiss ten bucks goodbye. Or she could buy tickets to one of the many shows. The ones she could afford were likely still more entertaining than slot machines that ate her quarters like Marian's dog ate kibble, and that supposition included the Engelbert Humperdinck imitators. She wished she could win something and afford tickets to Melissa or Madonna tonight.

Banish that thought, she told herself. Feeling desperate to win attracted losing. It wasn't logical, but it was true. She had her employer's hundred dollars, a gift for "research," Dana Moon had said. She was to spend it on blackjack, then write down every last impression she had of being an unskilled player at a middle stakes table. Dana's next thriller was a high stakes casino heist.

Ten minutes later, she tapped **Loser from Loserville, that's what it feels like** into her Blackberry. Swear to freakin' god, she'd never seen cards so bad. She'd been dealt twelve, three times in a row, and gotten a ten as the next card every time. Nobody busts with twenty-two three times in a row, ka-ching, ka-ching, ka-ching. The dealer had even looked a little chagrinned.

She glanced at her watch. Marian would be another hour at least. She would have gone along to watch her mostest favorite librarian participate on a panel discussion of cultural sensitivity in the labeling and display of young adult titles, but she was sort of more-or-less banned from the proceedings because of last year. Not *officially* banned, but really, that idiot guy had *so* not known what he was talking about, and in her opinion any librarian who supported a censorship position ought to go to work at the department of motor vehicles alphabetizing license plates.

Marian had tried to calm her down after the, uh, intense debate. Really, the people who called it an altercation had exaggerated. "Liddy, sweetie, I know you love to ask questions, and I have never seen anyone who loves a good debate like you—"

Liddy had snarled in the general direction of petty fascists the world over. "Debate? I was kicking his ass, and if he calls you *little lady* one more time, I'm gonna kick his ass for real."

"Sweetie, I know you feel strongly about it, and I know you really can kick his ass because I saw you get your black belt, but you can't go around kicking the asses of the members of the association's board. Especially when you're not a librarian and you aren't even a paid attendee at the conference."

When Marian was right, she was right, and Liddy had learned to accept it. And when she'd asked Liddy not to go into any of the sessions this year, and hinted she was just passing on a more or less official request, Liddy had promised to be good.

She wandered away from the slot machines and watched the roulette wheel spin and spin. Nobody was winning. Poor Marian—the panel was probably boring her out of her mind. She could hear her love right now explaining that librarians did not act *in loco parentis*, and that any so-called child with the wherewithal to find a book ought to be able to check that book out, and any parents who wanted to keep a firm grip on what their children were reading had the flawless recourse of not agreeing to give their children their own cards. It was that simple. But no, parents wanted to park their children at the library after school for a couple of hours, and then they got upset when their children actually *used* the library to look up stuff that interested them. Number one search for males aged twelve to eighteen was sex.

Number two: sex.

Number three: cars.

Number four: sex in cars.

The information you pick up as the girlfriend of a librarian was amazing.

Bored by the roulette wheel, she mosied toward a noisy craps gathering, but the moment she walked up the shooter lost. Wow—she was the kiss of death for everybody today.

So, she could see about making her next twenty dollars last an hour—unlikely—or she could think of something else to amuse herself.

Text messages were free, she thought. She punched up Marian's number and asked her if she was able to get texts.

Marian replied that her bit was over and she was seated in the audience and asked what was wrong, all with the economically phrased message, **Done, off dais, okay?**

Liddy texted back, **1 A walk in a thunderstorm.**

?

2 Your shirt soaked to your skin. There was no reply, and Liddy was pretty sure she had Marian's attention. **3 My shirt soaked to my skin.**

Well, maybe she should play a little bit more video poker. Her next twenty bucks lasted longer because she stopped after every dollar or so lost to send Marian another text.

4 Chasing drops of rain down your throat with my tongue. She quickly found that it was ill-advised to attempt to draw to an inside straight.

She had drawn a spade to go with four diamonds when a reply from Marian arrived.

She smiled fondly as she read: **5 You make love like you eat.**

Maybe she could find a pint of ice cream and a spoon and invite Marian upstairs for a memorable lunch. A couple of clicks on the poker machine brought her a modest return in the form of three of a kind. For ten minutes, she played happily, not quite losing, then her fortunes took another turn for the worse.

6 Against the door.

Immediately she got back: **7 You naked. Me not.**

She shivered. Five years and that still turned her on. Marian the Librarian was really playful, and the best part was nobody suspected, so there were no nympho-femmes trying to poach her girl. Liddy hadn't known she was a nympho-femme until Marian.

She looked down when her phone buzzed.

8 Shower?

9 Your favorite word, yes.

Marian didn't answer, so it was possible she had to actually talk to people or something. Liddy cashed out what was left of her money in the poker machine and carried the quarters to a good ol' Lucky 7 slot machine. Plink-plink-plink, spin-whirl-click, gone-gone-gone.

Maybe she should try a different casino, but she didn't want to leave. It was rather nice to have more women than men in the hotel, and there were librarians everywhere. Attendees for the Escort Services International group were also in evidence, and there were even some faces she recognized as famous romance writers.

Marian said that writers and librarians were natural pairings, and even if Liddy wasn't a writer, she did research for one, which made them even more ideal as mates. What Liddy couldn't find, Marian could. They'd lie in bed at night talking about search strings and cataloging, total geeks, then Marian would take off her glasses, take off Liddy's clothes, and in the morning there were towels and sheets to wash. Marian's favorite flannel sheets hadn't survived their first year.

Her phone buzzed.

10 All my fingers, all over you.

Well, okay, Liddy had started her little game thinking to make Marian crazy, but at the moment, Marian was getting the upper hand. She laughed, startling the man on the stool next to her. What else was new? Marian always had the upper hand, and they both really liked it that way. **11 plus your tongue.**

12 Our first night together, you.

Oh, Marian was not playing fair. Liddy abandoned the slot machine as the memories of that first night washed over her. She'd not known just how multi-orgasmic she could be. She'd not been that way with anyone else, and wonderful Marian had decided that just because Liddy didn't know she *could*, that wasn't the same as knowing she *couldn't*.

Marian, again. **13 the next day and night.**

Now she was just showing off. **14 hours it took you to call me after.**

15 times I've said sorry.

16 times I've said sorry for bringing it up. Oh dear, things were not going the way she intended.

17 Favorite thing: Make up sex?

Liddy laughed, relieved. Her steps turned toward the conference center. **18 Yes, please. Now.**

19 minutes I have left in this session.

20 minutes till I see you in our room.

21 this afternoon, you.

Liddy blushed and was so glad no one else could see the display. When Marian got in these moods and wanted to see how often Liddy could... Nympho-femme, she thought, and don't say that like it's a bad thing.

She sent back: **Game over. I've won all I need, all I want.**

"What I love," Marian whispered against Liddy's breasts, "is feeling like I make your fantasies come true."

Liddy was incredibly pleased with the status of the world, the cosmos, and the praline truffle ice cream that had not quite melted all the way. It had made for a wonderful snack before Marian decided they should shower and go back to bed. "You make fantasies come true that I didn't even know I had. That's the really amazing part."

"Want some more to come true?"

"Not right now—I mean, yes, actually." Liddy grinned at her lover.

"You have the most amazing eyes," Marian said. "The goddess was playing with the most beautiful blues and greens when she conceived you."

Liddy redirected Marian's hand from between her legs to her breast.

"If you don't want that, what do you want?" Marian tweaked Liddy's nipple, which responded as it always did even after the hours of fun.

"You." Liddy ruffled the short hair that curled ever so slightly on Marian's forehead. "You don't need the way I do, but I know that you need. I told you the first time we were together I wasn't a pillow queen."

"You never have been. That you let me play with you the way I do is one of the ways you make love to me."

Liddy tweaked Marian's nipple exactly the way Marian was touching hers. She'd learned that the confident lover who could be so aggressive and so thorough needed a few minutes to fade before a more vulnerable woman emerged, one who could let Liddy see her need.

Tapping into a patience she did not normally possess but had learned to nurture, Liddy stroked Marian's hair. They had already had five years of passion—passion for their work, their friends, each other. Learning to take and give had been so

183

important.

"We're going to miss out on baseball theme night," Marian said. Her playful tone was at odds with the need now showing in her eyes.

"Don't let me be selfish," Liddy whispered. "It's not good for me." She touched the tip of her tongue to Marian's earlobe, then rubbed her lips along Marian's cheek and jaw.

Marian exhaled, a small sound that Liddy knew was surrender to Liddy taking control. With a purr of pleasure, Liddy peeled Marian's T-shirt off, glad that the skittishness that she had first encountered when making love to Marian was long gone.

"I love you," she said, knowing Marian needed to hear it. She slid one arm under Marian's shoulders, pulling her close while her other hand explored the wonderful, full breasts. She wanted to say, "Beautiful," but Marian's gentle butch objected to the word. Instead, she held the word in her mouth as she kissed Marian slowly, luxuriously. No one had ever made her feel as if she could read minds, interpret the most subtle body language the way Marian did. It was a powerful feeling that sprang from intimacy, not the mind games they had both endured in their exes.

Marian loved her touch, and it still went right to her head, a different kind of dizzy arousal than what she'd already experienced. She stayed close, drowning them both in kisses while her hand finally dipped between Marian's legs. The explosion of wetness made her whimper. She drenched her fingers with it, brought them to her mouth, tasted and licked, then painted Marian's lips with the wonderful essence. More kisses, her fingers again dipping, pressing, then finally, sliding inside.

"Oh, yes." Marian arched into their kisses, shuddering under Liddy's hand.

"I'm right here, darling." Liddy breathed out the

reassurance, felt it unknot the tension in Marian's shoulders, spreading down her body until her legs parted. She was suddenly so wet that Liddy's hand was swimming. "I know this is what you need."

She pressed inward, smooth and steady, drawing a hoarse, sharp cry out of Marian that turned into an ecstatic, exultant, "Yes!"

My favorite word too, Liddy thought. Our favorite word.

After a few minutes of increasingly languid kisses and murmured reassurances, Liddy smooched away the faint hint of tears in the corners of Marian's eyes. "Love you, and I love doing that to you."

"Baseball night," Marian mumbled. "We're missing out."

"Sleep." She watched Marian's eyelids droop.

"But you wanted to gamble."

"Don't need to. I'm already the winner." Marian's hand tightened on hers, then slowly went limp. Liddy smiled into Marian's hair, and after one more sigh of contentment, joined her in sleep.

Just Like That

Published: 2005
Characters: Syrah Ardani, vintner
                Toni Blanchard, financier
                Anthony Ardani, vintner
                Bennett, factotum
Setting: Napa Valley, California

Seventeen is Prime Time

The Beautiful Expression of
Her Dark Eyes

(5 years)

She was late for Missy Bingley's and Jane Lucas's anniversary party. This fact mattered not at all to Toni Blanchard. Far more importantly, as she sat in Friday evening traffic streaming out of San Francisco and into the soft summer Napa evening, was that Missy's and Jane's anniversary was also her own. And she was late.

The lazy Napa sun was so low it seemed to drape over the coastal hills, dusting translucent orange silk over the rolling fields and the surface of Toni's convertible windscreen. The evening breeze, which rose when the sun set, tickled at her temples. Inching along at less than five miles an hour she was busy doing things a person shouldn't while driving—pulling toiletries out of her suitcase, stripping the ties out of her braid

189

and brushing it out, sponging off make-up she'd put on almost fourteen hours ago in Minnesota. She wanted to be clean.

Clean, and human. She wanted out of her suit, away from cars and fumes and even the small shops that lined the center of the small town. She wanted to be in Syrah's fields, rolling a grape between her fingers and listening to her love tell her why that grape would—or wouldn't—someday be poetry in a glass.

She would watch Syrah crush a grape and smell it, touch it to the tip of her tongue and inhale, then bite off about half the fruit and mash it against her upper palate as her eyes closed. "This will be early September," she'd say. Or she'd shake her head and murmur, "I still taste the last year's dry summer."

Syrah would guide Toni's hand to the base of the vine, explaining its lineage the way a trainer would describe a thoroughbred's pedigree. Toni adored Syrah's hands, always slightly dry, fingertips so sensitive. Her touch never failed to send warm, delicious tendrils of desire along her arms.

Eventually Syrah would say, "You're not really listening."

"Every word, I heard every word," Toni always answered.

"Oh yeah? What's the last thing I said?"

If she'd been listening, Toni would recount the last few words. If she'd been instead focused on Syrah's fingers, the graceful arch of her wrist, the memory of the night in these fields when Syrah had first overwhelmed her senses, she'd kiss her as an answer.

More often than not, she'd kiss her, even if she had been listening.

But for the traffic she would have closed her eyes and recalled any of the dozen times they had fallen together into the shadow of the leafy vines. In spite of their jeans and Ardani vineyard work shirts, they became two women loving each other as simply and naturally as any might have hundreds of years ago under Bordeaux or Provence skies. Though surrender in the bedroom had never been easy for Toni, with Syrah, among the vines, she found it easy to let Syrah's sensuality wrap them both in the cocoon of love.

C'mon Toni, she chided herself. Cocoon of love? How many of her New York friends would be begging her to stop right there? But it wasn't her fault. Syrah's father had put it best: "Wine makes poets of us all. Maybe not *good* poets, but *happy* ones."

She laughed into the rearview mirror. The deep lines around her eyes revealed her as anything but happy. She ached all over, her stomach was queasy in spite of her feeling echoingly hollow and if she let herself, she'd cry in a heartbeat.

Probably would before her anniversary was over.

Ten minutes and three waits through the central square's stoplight later, she turned off the main drag and headed for a less direct and much faster route toward the Ardani vineyard. Five years ago she'd been put out by the use of country roads when a perfectly good freeway was available. No more—she'd learned every possible alternative.

Learned, too, that most of the time in a vineyard was spent waiting. Crews came and went, barrels were rotated, all routine. All in due time. All in measured steps. Then the grapes came on to ripen in September and October and the pace was frenetic. Frenzied harvest, trucks from other growers everywhere, grapes they were keeping loaded into the first presses for crushing and everyone and everything sticky with grape juice.

Kisses were tart, hurried, lovemaking frantic and needy.

"I'm too tired to sleep," Syrah had said at one point last year. They'd showered and fallen into bed.

Rolling over, Toni had lost herself in the beautiful expression of her dark eyes, just the way she had the moment they'd met. Shivering, she had buried her lips in the hollow of Syrah's throat, whispering, "Let me put you to sleep, darling."

Syrah's groan had inflamed her further and words spilled around them. At first they were endearments, then short, sharp explosions that finally lost form but not meaning. Toni had felt drunk with the knowledge of her lover's body. Time had ripened them both. She knew the shudder, heard the need, was fast and hard. Fast and hard until Syrah had shivered with a more profound exhaustion and tumbled into sleep, leaving Toni to listen to the slowing heartbeat against her ear.

Left, right, stop sign, turns and double-backs as complicated as a maze, but every turn took her further from work and closer to home.

She'd warned Syrah that the negotiations might drag on. Explained she might miss their anniversary. Syrah had gone to Missy's and Jane's alone, but a party at Netherfield was always an event. Missy and Jane oozed happiness, brimmed with good cheer, their lives one day of bliss after another. She'd once told Missy that they were so sweet together they should provide guests with insulin.

Missy's narrow-gazed retort had been, "As if everyone who visits you and Syrah doesn't need a cold shower after ten minutes."

She'd been glad to check out of the residence hotel where she'd been living out of her suitcase for the last month. She'd exhausted every possible entertainment available in Cokato Minnesota and its surrounds. She'd even been to the Corn Festival. Twice in one weekend.

All for naught.

Treacherous thoughts had not crossed her mind until the door slammed behind the last party to leave the table but her. She couldn't let it. She was utterly and totally committed to a workout of some kind. But the moment it had irrevocably fallen out of reach she had thought, "I can go home now. Thank God, because I hate this."

Her admin team had worked wonders finding her a flight,

having a rental car waiting, but they couldn't do anything about the damned traffic. What she had hoped would be a surprise arrival in time for the party had turned to a hope to surprise Syrah before the sun set. It was three-quarters hidden by the hills now.

There was only a sliver of golden disk left when she turned in to the gate and gunned the rental up the hill to the house. The kitchen lights were on, and so were the lights in Syrah's father's rooms in the front of the upper floor. Their room was dark. Perhaps Syrah was still at the party.

She left her suitcase and jacket in the car. Stiff, almost limping with fatigue, she walked around to the kitchen door.

She wasn't even through the door when Bennett, hands on her hips, barked, "About time!"

"It's so good to be home." The warmth and soft lights of the Ardani kitchen was like a balm on her bruised spirits.

Bennett thrust a wedge of crusty bread at her. It was slathered with a soft cheese and dotted with diced sun-dried tomatoes. "Syrah's been like a cat on a hot tin roof for a week. Got back from the party a bit ago and went for a walk. Restless, like always when you're not here. I don't know what could possibly be so fascinating about corn and it's vexing that—"

"She went toward the chardonnays and building four." Anthony Ardani leaned against the doorjamb, a relaxed smile of welcome lighting up his gentle face.

Toni finished the treat Bennett had given her in four bites. Her stomach immediately settled. "Thank you, sir."

"I'm glad you're home. You've been missed."

Bennett harrumphed. "Indeed, no one with a sensible clue about a good diet when you're not here. Syrah will be getting fat one of these days. And himself," she added as she turned back to her cutting board with a sniff. "It's cheese every meal and twice that on Sundays. Finally have someone around who appreciates a proper salad."

"I don't care what you make, Bennett dear, as long as it's not corn."

She left the familiar, comforting bickering behind, regretting her high heels and hose as she made her way over the gravel drive in the direction Anthony had suggested. She passed building four with no sign of Syrah, so turned back to the vines she thought were the chardonnays.

All that was left of the sun was a glow of sharp yellow that softened to burnt orange, then deepened to a crystal blue. The evening star winked into sight and she realized that the moon was rising. It would be a beautiful Napa Valley night.

She caught the distant sound of humming on the breeze and turned toward it, knowing the tuneless murmurs. More confident now, she followed a downward slope. The vines were fully leaved and she was sure there were healthy clusters hiding under those leaves, but with day fading and night coming on her eyes were only for the outline of the woman at the end of the next row.

She was, and always was, exactly as Toni remembered her, only better. How had she ever thought Syrah unremarkable? Walking in her fields Syrah was a dancer in jeans and muddy boots. She touched her grapes like they were precious lovers. So close, not yet seen, Toni ached for Syrah's touch. Wanted to be enclosed, sensed, felt, measured and loved.

Syrah saw her.

The moonlight carried that look and all in that moment Toni felt claimed by those dark eyes and by the soft smile of wonder and relief.

"Happy anniversary. I'm sorry I'm late."

"Don't be silly. You must have bought an airline to get here so quickly." Syrah held out her hands.

She must have walked down the row, but didn't remember it. All she felt was the warmth of Syrah's fingertips and a wave of pleasure at the touch of their hands. "The ticket price should have made me a major shareholder, but that's not the way it works."

Syrah gazed at her, then said simply, "Welcome back."

"I don't want to leave, ever again."

With that she started to cry, tried and failed to stop the tears, and then was a mess of gulping sobs. The hard-boiled corporate workout specialist—right. Undone by poetry in a glass and the love of a good woman.

Syrah settled down on the ground, vines to her back, and pulled at Toni to join her. Cradled against Syrah's shoulder, she managed to get herself under control, but it took a while.

After offering the underside of her T-shirt for the purpose of wiping Toni's eyes, Syrah said, "I take it things didn't go well."

Toni shook her head. "One hundred and seventeen jobs. Nobody wanted a pay cut and so nobody has a job. The investors didn't want less than all their money back so they're going to get next to none of it. It's on the auction block next week, as already ordered by the court. Item: one corn processing and packing plant, vacant."

"It takes so much out of you." Syrah gave her a squeeze.

Toni could hear the low, steady beating of Syrah's heart. "Well, there's been a lot more failures than successes for the last two years."

"Do you really want to give up?"

"And what will my staff do?"

"Open their own firms?"

Toni sighed. They'd been through it all before. She enjoyed the work when it went well. But when it went badly she wanted to sink her fingers into the vineyard dirt and listen to Syrah's heartbeat. "I felt like such crap and then Bennett—"

"Gave you a snack, chewed on your ear and now you're better?"

A tiny smile threatened. Bennett's food, Syrah's eyes...

miracle cures. "She's a kitchen witch—and I mean that in the best sense of the word."

"You're so lucky, because I don't cook."

"Neither do I."

"You have other talents." Syrah's lips brushed over Toni's brow.

The skin across her chest tingled and then an enveloping warmth spread over her breasts and stomach. "So do you."

Syrah tipped her head back and kissed her softly, then again with more intent, and again with rising heat.

Toni turned fully into her embrace, yielding. The depth of her abandon had once frightened her, but now she reveled in Syrah's strength even as her hands explored all of the soft, full curves of Syrah's body.

At times like this Toni thought they shouldn't be so close to the vines. The heat between them was so intense she was surprised they didn't singe the grapes. She slipped her hands under Syrah's shirt and was completely undone at the soft, voluptuous welcome. The smell of fresh earth, the scent of growing things and a sensuous woman—they were better than any drug could be. And they were hers.

She loved the little sounds that Syrah made. Lost in their kisses, she wasn't aware of Syrah's hand slipping under her skirt until the pressure of fingertips sent a shockwave down her legs.

"Please," she whispered. There was no reason not to yield. They were alone in the world, surrounded by beauty, and the moon was rising.

If Anthony noticed the dirt on Toni's suit, he didn't mention it. She ran up the stairs to change and was back down in time to catch the ripening scent of the lovely varietal table red that Anthony had uncorked.

"To my two daughters," he said, lifting his glass. "To married life, and to the grapes!"

"To the grapes," Toni echoed. She caught Syrah's hand, kissed her lightly and was home again, sipping poetry from a glass.

Finders Keepers

Published:	2006
Characters:	Marissa Chabot, online dating consultant
	Linda Bartok, traveler
Setting:	A not-so-deserted isle in the South Pacific
	East Bay, California

Nineteen, on the edge

Gladiators

(1 year)

"Half the women on board are going to think you're her at first." Marissa surveyed Linda's gladiator costume, complete with breastplate and rubber sword. Given the cheerful ocean motif of the wallpaper and paintings that brightened their spacious suite, it was incongruous to say the least. Which didn't mean it wasn't very attractive, she thought. It was. Her lover was built to carry off that entire look.

Linda struck the famous warrior pose, using every inch of her nearly six feet to menacingly arc her sword overhead. "It doesn't bother me anymore. Besides…"

Without warning she dropped the weapon and tumbled Marissa onto the luxurious kind-sized bed. "You are most definitely not some featherweight sidekick everyone wishes was really my girlfriend."

"Got that right. I am most definitely your girlfriend, and I'm no featherweight."

Linda kissed her and Marissa happily took note that it was not a light, bouncy I-love-you kiss, and not a later-let's-do-more kiss. It was a let's-turn-on-all-the-lights-and-take-off-all-our-clothes kiss.

When she was able, Marissa said, "I just got into these stockings."

"Are you really going to make me wait?" She was treated to another kiss with one of those patented dark-eyed looks where Marissa could see herself in the depths.

"Our dinner seating begins in fifteen minutes."

"Why did we go for the early seating?" Linda planted little kisses all around Marissa's collarbone.

"We wanted to be sure to have time for a nightly walk on the deck before going to bed."

"Mmm. Bed." Linda continued with the little kisses, moving down the deep cleavage of Marissa's servant-of-the-temple costume.

"And so far, my dear Ms. Bartok, we've gone to bed every night without taking a walk."

"And, my dear Ms. Chabot, we still achieved highly aerobic activity with sustained target heart rates."

Marissa giggled. "Brown-eyed woman."

"Are you saying I'm full of shit?"

Marissa's quip died on her lips as she touched Linda's hair where it brushed her shoulders. The dark strands moved like silk against her fingertips and for just a moment she was back in the island bungalow where they had first made love, experiencing the magic of Linda's touch, feeling wanted and sensual for the first time in her life.

"Hey." Linda's gaze was gentle and open. "Where'd you go?"

"I was thinking about Tahiti." The pain of all that had happened after that night had been washed over with the promise of their future. Where she had once dreaded each new day without Linda, now she welcomed every sunrise. "Thank you for loving me."

"Are you kidding?" Linda moved off Marissa, settling along her side. "That was the best night of my life."

Marissa could have spent the next hour like this, quietly talking about whatever came to mind, and reveling in the little sensations, like the warmth of Linda's cheek against her fingertips. They both worked too hard and rarely had time like this together. "The *first* best night of your life, you mean."

Linda grinned again. "I stand corrected." She leaned in for a kiss, but the breastplate got in the way. When a strap popped and a point dug into Marissa's forearm, Linda acknowledged defeat.

"Okay, we'll wait. But I am going to liberate you from your days as a temple slave." She clambered off the bed to fix her breastplate strap.

"And I'll be just your slave after that?"

"Of course." Linda wiggled in a circle as she tried to adjust the pleated leather skirt. "I plan to have my way with you."

"Let me." Marissa slipped both hands up Linda's skirt and found the hem of the undershirt. With a little tug she got rid of the rumple. Then, just for good measure, she gave Linda's backside a very friendly squeeze.

"Liking your slave duties already?"

Marissa answered with a sharp swat. "You have to help me get my bra on correctly."

"Gladly." Linda posed in the narrow mirror with her sword. "The skirt looks perfect now. Thanks."

Marissa slipped the gathered straps of the diaphanous gown off her shoulders.

Linda made a show of tossing her sword to one side. "How

can I help with the presentation of your boobages?"

Marissa gave Linda a dour look, which Linda ignored as usual, and then turned her back. "Tighten the hooks and then when I've got everything lifted, you're going to tighten these silly clear straps so everything stays. You know, the package says it's for the full-figured gal, but not one with shoulders."

Linda adjusted the hooks as Marissa had asked, then kissed Marissa between the shoulder blades. "And have you got shoulders. Free weight heaven."

Marissa looked at Linda's reflection in the mirror. "I could care less about the weights. But it felt really good to heave my own carry-on into the overhead bin. If I am ever on a sinking ship again I'll be the first one out, and I'll be able to help other people too." She lifted the bra cups so the straps had more slack. "Tighten please."

The sword was retrieved and sheathed and last minute fixes to hair achieved, then they were ready for costume night dinner, a la the Italian cruise line's design. Marissa thought it great fun to dress up, and was glad Linda had made peace with her unnatural resemblance to the real warrior princess.

Just as she opened the door, Linda reached into the small refrigerator in the suite's bar area. "For my beautiful slave girl. A slave no more."

"Oh, Linda." Touched, Marissa took the simple crown of laurel leaves wrapped around florist wire. She snipped off the little tag from the ship's florist. "It makes the costume perfect."

"Allow me," Linda said. Marissa bent her head and felt the cool touch of the leaves all around her scalp. "My divine lady."

She blushed. Sometimes she still caught herself not believing that Linda saw her as beautiful. When Linda made it clear with such romantic gestures, she still felt surprised. Linda pulled her close and they shared a soft, very tender kiss. It was a few minutes before they made their way out of their cabin.

"Okay, so we're in the minority for costumes." Marissa held Linda's hand as they approached the dining room.

There was a smattering of women in similar white-gowned garb to her own, but most of the other women were in casual evening clothes. Linda, in her full warrior regalia, was attracting quite a lot of attention, but that was nothing new. She took it in stride and Marissa wanted to tell Linda how proud she was that the attention no longer sent her running to the ends of the earth. The warm hand she held reflected none of the tension that had been present when they'd first met, when a remark about Linda's resemblance to glamorous heroines of stage and screen caused Linda a great deal of anguish.

"That sword should be a Chakram," a petite blonde observed as they waited for the maitre d's attention.

Linda patted the breastplate. "Chakram's under here."

Stepping well into Linda's personal space, the blonde said coquettishly, "Can I see?"

Marissa arched one eyebrow. Blondie didn't see that Linda was holding hands with someone already?

"Sorry," Linda said easily. "I've already got a Gabrielle."

With a flutter of eyelashes the blonde moved on.

"Oh the travails of fame and fortune," Marissa said. She nodded at the maitre d' and followed him across the main floor of the restaurant.

Linda pulled out Marissa's chair and they greeted the other three couples at their table. The day spent cruising and lounging was evident in a number of near sunburns, but one couple had had some success in the casino.

"We tried yesterday," Linda said. "Blew our budget in about two hours."

"Cat's lucky with cards." Marissa could not remember the speaker's name, only that she and her partner lived in San Francisco. "Now we can buy more souvenirs for the grandkids."

Cat gave her partner a mock scolding glance. "Jess, we're not grandmothers, remember?"

"Yes, dear."

Marissa chuckled appreciatively. Someday she hoped to be just as comfortable and indulgently affectionate with Linda as Cat and Jessica were with each other. They'd even had a child together and now were grandparents. Kids weren't in her and Linda's plans, not yet anyway, even if Marissa's mother was agitating in the worst possible fashion.

An uproar at the door brought all conversation to a halt. With a stamp of feet and clash of very real looking swords, female crew members in full gladiatorial regalia marched into the dining room, flushed and giggling. Their breastplates bore the colors of the Italian flag, and many had a face more red than her costume.

"They never get to do the march," Cat yelled over the din. "This week the cruise organizers made the captain make an exception. Woo!" She began swinging her napkin over her head and soon everyone followed suit.

The cheering screams as the gladiators circled the room were deafening. Linda stamped her feet as Marissa tried to yell herself hoarse. Impossibly, the bedlam escalated at the promised presentation of Bacchus. A chaise appeared carried on the shoulders of toga-clad men, but instead of the god Bacchus, it was the woman who owned the touring company, wrapped scantily in a toga and bearing the sign, *Sappho*.

After the chaise made a circuit, "Sappho" stepped off to thank her bearers and made a little speech ending with "More wine!"

The cheering resumed as the gladiators exited the dining

room and calmed somewhat as the pianist launched into "That's Amore!"

"Sounds like plenty of wine has already been had," Linda said as other diners began singing along with the music.

Jessica grinned. "It's high spirits. It's been such a great week so far and we all get to be who we are. Ten percent of the new millenium is over and we still need places where we know it's safe to be free."

"It's been a real reminder to me that not everybody gets to live where we live." Marissa smiled. "We're very lucky there."

"I met this adorable couple from Topeka and they are on Cloud Nine. One woman doesn't know how they'll be able to go back to the so-called real world."

The waiter offered them the daily menu and she and Linda quickly agreed on what they'd split and share. By then the pianist had segued to "It's a Small World" and the high-spirited crowd quickly adapted the lyrics.

Linda chortled and joined in. "It's a gay, gay world!"

Dinner was a blur to Marissa. There were so many good pheromones in the room and the wine was wonderful—it all felt like something out of a dream. But most wonderful was the way she felt about Linda. The last year had been as heavenly as the first year had not. They both worked hard but every day, at least once a day, they said *I love you* and found a way to make the other laugh. They made love sometimes in quick little bursts of release and other times set aside a long afternoon to explore each other.

By dessert, though she'd only had one glass of wine, she felt tipsy. But when Linda tried to guide them down the stairs to their suite, she instead insisted on a walk around the deck. "Come on, the dessert was decadent. There's later, sweetheart."

Linda indulged her and they walked toward the bow, sheltered from the wind until they reached the foredeck. A good-sized barrier prevented them from going into the bow but the wind was refreshing and it cleared Marissa's head. By the time they'd made a complete circuit she felt much more focused but the tingles of wonder and awe every time she looked at Linda were just as strong.

Out of the wind on the aft deck above the pool, she leaned into Linda and pointed out the rising moon. "Remember that beautiful moon in Tahiti? The sea was so still that it looked like a magical pathway over the surface would let us walk right to it."

"I have to say I'm really happy to be on a ship that has stayed afloat."

Marissa squeezed Linda's arm. "Me too, even though I got what I wanted and needed out of that experience."

"Yeah?" Linda gazed down at her and Marissa recognized the only shadow that ever existed in Linda's eyes.

"Don't," Marissa said. No matter how often she told Linda she forgave her for that long, painful year when Linda had dropped out of her life without a word, Linda sometimes needed to be reassured. "It's okay."

"I could have sent a postcard from New Zealand, or an e-mail from any Internet café in Boston. I could have told you the truth before we left Tahiti, even."

"It's okay," Marissa repeated. "The hurt is long gone."

The shadow lessened but it hadn't entirely left Linda's eyes. "I want to spend the rest of my life making it up to you."

"Okay," Marissa said easily. "Sounds like you want to get married."

"I do."

A little silence fell and Marissa's heart was suddenly beating like she had just finished a half-hour on a stair stepper. Linda reached into the little waist pouch that Marissa had thought purely decorative and extracted something very thin.

"I'm not perfect, Marissa."

"I don't care if you're perfect or not." Her voice broke. "All that matters is that you're perfect for me and you think I'm perfect for you."

"Marry me. Please."

"Yes." Marissa's chin quivered and she looked down at what Linda had in the palm of her hand.

"When we get home we'll pick out real rings. But for now…"

She gently pushed a woven ring of blue fabric onto Marissa's ring finger. It was a little thick but even through a veil of tears, Marissa thought it was beautiful.

"I made it out of what was left of that scrap I carried to remind me of you. A real ring will replace it, I promise."

She threw herself into Linda's arms. "Yes, darling, yes. I want forever with you."

Linda swung her in a circle, setting her down to kiss her hungrily. "Let's go back to our room."

"We'll miss the jazz trio."

"Don't care."

Marissa was already leading Linda into the atrium. "Neither do I."

Her reflection, the woman she was, was bright and clear in Linda's eyes. The lights were on, all of them.

Linda had already exchanged her costume for an old soft T-shirt featuring a small cartoon of a dog with a snorkel in its mouth. Marissa blinked back tears, recalling all the nights she'd kept thaT-shirt under her pillow. Linda stretched out on the bed, one long, lean line, and watched Marissa remove her sandals, then roll down and carefully remove her thigh-high stockings.

Marissa no longer felt awkward undressing in front of Linda. A year and then some of proof that Linda got very excited just looking at her in anticipation of the moment Marissa slipped naked into her arms had given her the confidence to take her time. She sat down on the bed so Linda could reach her zipper and bra and without prompting, Linda undid both.

"Thank you." The gown had already slipped from her shoulders when she rose and she held it to the front of her as she removed her watch and bracelet, then her earrings. She didn't know if the exposed curve of her back and hint that the dress would fall to the ground if she let go was anyone's definition of sexy. All that mattered was that her body made Linda's gaze follow her with hunger and desire.

"You're teasing me."

"Am I?" Marissa let the gown slide to her waist and she slowly removed her bra.

"You know you are."

"Is there something you'd rather I do?" She let her bra fall from her fingers and shimmied the dress further down until it rested just at her hips.

"God, no."

"I don't want my dress to wrinkle." Turning her back, she lowered the dress until she could step out of it. She would bet money Linda's gaze was on the white silk panties she wore and she smiled to herself. No one had ever made her feel as powerfully attractive. She hung the dress in the closet and finally turned around. Linda had taken off the T-shirt and for a moment Marissa couldn't breathe.

"*Yummy-yum-yum.* Worth waiting for."

Recovering her wits she crossed the short distance to the bed. "One last thing to take off."

"Need help with that?"

"Oh yes." Marissa adopted her best impression of a Southern belle. "Why, I just can't figure out how to take them off all by my little lonesome."

"It's easy." Linda practically purred as she slid to the edge of the bed. "You use your teeth."

Linda's unrestrained intensity never failed to melt Marissa's confidence into an ache of desire. No longer the stalking tigress, she felt abruptly the prey. Linda first nipped at her thigh before she bit into the front of her panties and pulled them down. Marissa cupped Linda's face as heat from Linda's breath seemed to float over her entire body. With a shiver of delight she helped lower her panties until they pooled around her ankles and she could kick them off. Linda opened her arms and Marissa settled into the shelter of their encircling strength.

Breasts, stomachs, and thighs melted together as knees sorted themselves out with the ease of familiarity. The scratch of Linda's nails along the inside of one thigh drew a low moan from the back of Marissa's throat.

"Is this what you want, Marissa?"

She nodded, gaze locked with Linda's. When Linda dipped between her legs Marissa felt herself falling into the well of Linda's eyes. Entwined on their sides, Linda seemed intent on kissing Marissa until morning while her fingertips teased lightly. It was as languid as their lovemaking had been feverish the night before. With each new kiss and whispered affection Marissa grew more and more frantic for Linda's touch inside her.

"I love the way you can move for me," Linda whispered. Her hand shifted and Marissa felt the long, welcome stroke of her fingers. "I love the way your body feels against mine."

With a sudden, delicious spasm Marissa arched hard against Linda. The layers of sensation that radiated out from Linda's hand brought a tingle of electricity wherever her skin touched Linda's. There were stars behind her eyes, then all of that light folded inward until she glowed from the inside out.

"We could go to the lip sync contest," Marissa offered sleepily quite some time later.

"Sure."

Marissa knew that voice. Linda was asleep, but her brain's autopilot would mumble appropriate responses if Marissa kept talking.

"Will you get me a space shuttle for my birthday?"

"Sure."

Marissa laughed softly to herself, then rose to turn out the lights. She studied the sweep of Linda's hair over the pillow before faint moonlight from the porthole replaced the lamp's last glow.

She slipped back into the circle of Linda's arms and melted at the warmth of Linda behind her. "Go dancing with me tomorrow night?"

"Sure."

"Marry me?"

"Sure."

"Love me forever?"

"Abso-freaking-lutely."

"You're not asleep."

"I was."

Marissa fondly tickled the arm around her waist. "Thank you."

"For what?"

"All the tomorrows."

Linda pulled her a little closer. "Finders keepers, sweetheart. You're mine now."

Making Up For Lost Time

Published: 1998
Characters: Jamie Onassis, master chef
               Valkyrie Valentine, home repair expert
Setting: San Francisco and Mendocino California

The Eighth is for Eternity

Peanut Butter Toffee Cookies

Preheat oven to 350 F. You'll need two mixing bowls, mixer or sturdy spatula and a good arm, and ungreased cookie sheets.

1.5 cups of smooth or chunky peanut butter
1 cup butter
1 cup each sugar and packed light brown sugar
2 eggs
2.5 cups ordinary flour
2 tsp baking soda
1/4 tsp each baking powder and salt
10 oz of toffee bits

Bowl 1
Whip the butters until fluffy, then slowly beat in sugars until smooth. Add the eggs one at a time, mixing until well blended.

Bowl 2
Sift together the flour, baking soda, baking powder and salt. Slowly mix into the batter in bowl 1. Once incorporated, add the toffee bits to bowl 1 and stir together well.

Cookie Sheets
Drop heaping tablespoons of the batter onto cookie sheets, leaving at least one inch between each cookie. Flatten with chilled fork. Chewy cookies? Bake for 10 minutes. Crunchy? Bake for 12 minutes. Makes about 3 dozen.

 *From the Waterview, Mendocino*

Happy New Year Too

(10 years)

"Don't look at me that way. You know this is the way it has to be."

For the third morning in a row, the puppy scratched outside the kitchen door of the Waterview Inn. Jamie didn't know how long it had been on the streets—not long from the looks of the glossy brown and white spotted coat, and healthy, trimmed nails. Puppy was maybe not quite the right word, either. It was female, had a spay scar and was probably more than a year old, but not by much.

She didn't know her breeds well, but enough to know this dog was no pedigreed creature. As she told Val on the phone, it was a lot like the "lady dog" from *Lady and the Tramp*, but lacked the curly tendrils around the ears. The muzzle wasn't quite the same as her cartoon memory, either.

"You can't let it in," Val had warned her. "No animals in the restaurant."

"I know," Jamie had answered. She'd always had a soft spot for dogs, but Aunt Emily had never kept pets—same problem. It would be impossible to keep it out of the kitchen with their floor plan, and health inspectors would spot one in a surprise inspection. Shutting a dog up in a bedroom or office by itself for the better part of every day, especially a young, larger one used to space, seemed cruel to her.

She looked down at the puppy and sighed. It wagged its tail, big brown eyes shiny and bright, and looked at her as if she were the sum total of its entire reason to exist. Sometimes, that was exactly the way Val looked at her, but Val was taping her latest season of *A Month of Sundays* and hadn't been home in over two months now, and it was still four weeks until Jamie went to New York for Thanksgiving.

She loved that her Val was the beloved hottie do-it-yourself queen Valkyrie Valentine. And they both loved the Waterview Inn and the little town of Mendocino too, the place where Jamie had grown up. Val had worked hard to make the Inn a showplace of relaxed elegance that was a "must-see" in tourist guides for the Northern California coast, while Jamie lived out her passion for food creating bistro and homey fare for locals and travelers. The problem was that Val's network's studio and the Waterview Inn were three thousand miles apart.

On the fourth morning she couldn't stand it—the puppy definitely looked thinner and hungrier. A bowl of basic scraps and another of water was the humane thing to do. She put them at the very far end of the mud porch where the dog could come and go at will, and cursed tourists. Undoubtedly, someone had been traveling with the little sweetheart and either dumped it or it had gotten lost. They'd gone on their way and left the dog.

It was way off season now, and the chances of tourists coming back to remote Mendocino to look were slim to none. She'd post signs, though, just in case. The town was emptier every day as the other shop owners and locals headed to their winter haunts, so finding a home would be difficult.

Her "aunt" Liesel already had one such adopted dog, and Jamie got to pet Stubby several times a week. No doubt when she walked down to Liesel's house for their Thursday night dinner, Stubby would be very intrigued by the aroma of another dog on Jamie's pant legs. Maybe Liesel wanted another pet. Maybe she wouldn't have to call the humane society.

When Val called for their afternoon chat, just before dinner New York time, Jamie didn't tell her about the dog. Well, about feeding the dog. Val would stress about it, and say Jamie was headed down a slippery slope and she'd be right, and New York was really far away some nights.

"What shall we do for Christmas this year, honey?" It sounded like Val was sprawled across the ridiculous fuchsia fainting couch in the bedroom of the Greenwich Village loft. Her apartment was the occasional scene of a background shoot, and Val's own renovations combined with her network's designer had turned the place into a showpiece fit for Valkyrie Valentine, the woman-who-can-do-it-all. Val had hated that fainting couch until a memorable evening during one of Jamie's visits.

"Hawaii? It'll be warm and sunny, and we'd get tans to bring back to the fog. I can't leave until the fifteenth, though. The first through the fifteenth is my stint for checking the merchant premises for problems."

"Have there been any issues so far?"

"No—no signs of squatters, though Whispering Pines had an upper door blow open. Jacob spotted it." Jamie decided the piece of shortbread closest to her was far too ragged to sell, so she broke it in two and devoured half. The longer Val was away, the more sweets she consumed. "So what do you think of Hawaii?"

"That's tempting, very tempting. There are also great rentals on the French southern coast. You practically don't even have to cook—fresh fruit and veg and cheese and wine, just waiting for the picnic basket and the local markets."

Jamie heard the telltale scratch at the door. "Just when there's so little fresh here too—that sounds really good. Shall we flip a coin?"

"I'd rather flip you."

Ten years and she was still susceptible to the purr in Val's voice. She was about to suggest Val call her later, around bedtime maybe, when there was another scratch at the door. Sexy partner on phone and the adorable stray puppy vied for her focus. "That's sounding really good right now. I can't wait for Thanksgiving."

There was a short, sharp bark from the mud porch. Jamie peered out the screen and made a stern face. The puppy wagged its tail so hard it nearly fell over.

"Just you make sure there's no fog."

"No dog...fog. No fog. It hasn't been that bad for two years, so you can bet I'll be on that plane."

Val said a bad word, then, "Sorry, sweetie. Doorbell. I think it's Sheila and some phenom she's been trying to get a guest spot for. Some *Top Chef* finalist."

Jamie grinned into the phone. "Not from the show you guest judged?"

"Don't think so. Hang on."

Jamie could hear Val's side of a conversation, then the unmistakable cloying tones of Sheila's voice, though she couldn't make out the words. She never would like Sheila much, though she had grown to tolerate her over the last ten years.

"Sure—I haven't eaten yet. No, let me finish talking to my girl. There's wine. You know where." Into the phone, "I guess we're going out to dinner. She has a table at Craft booked."

"You lucky dog!"

"I will show you better at Thanksgiving, sweetie."

"I should hope you'd show me better than anything Sheila sees."

Val's voice plummeted to its most husky colors. "Why don't I call you when I get in?"

Jamie made her I-just-bit-into-chocolate-and-it's-melting-in-my-mouth sound. "It's a date."

Two sharp barks interrupted their goodbyes.

"What was that?"

Jamie could hear Val's arched eyebrow through the phone. "Not sure. You call me, don't forget."

She hung up hurriedly and slipped out onto the mud porch. "You can't do that. There's no barking when Val's on the phone. Got it?"

The lady dog puppy shivered all over, one big bag of wiggling rapturous Jell-O love.

Maybe she was lonely, and maybe she was a sucker for big brown eyes, but she got down on her knees and scratched the ears and chest and allowed a big slurp across her nose. It really didn't matter why. She fetched an old rug and made sure the water dish was full.

"Liesel's going to be here for all the folks dropping in to pick up their pies. That is, if I actually get to leave in the morning. Which doesn't seem likely. There are no tourists, either, so no Thanksgiving week bump because of it." Jamie cradled the phone on her shoulder as she savagely scraped whipped cream out of the copper bowl. "It's pea soup out

219

there, and I'm not kidding, Val. I can't see the other side of the street. It's that eerie quiet—no cars, no sound of the ocean, no gull calls even."

"I'm so sorry, honey." Val's voice was reedy on the line, and she sounded as if she were calling from the moon. "I hate this more every year. I hate being here half the year, and you there."

"Lifestyles of the rich and famous." Jamie agreed completely with what Val was saying, but there was little point in complaining about what she couldn't change. "I want to be there tomorrow night. I want to wake up Thanksgiving morning next to you. I'm not exaggerating the damned fog."

She didn't glance out the window again. If she did, she'd start to cry and she didn't like to cry on the phone with Val. The cure for it was Val's arms around her and that wasn't going to happen, so crying was no good. She muffled a sniff.

"I know you're not. Maybe I can get there."

"You'd have to be back Sunday evening, and you're even worse driving in the fog than I am. Jacob says it's all the way to Willits going inland, and doesn't break until Bodega Bay going south. The market has a sign up that trucking shipments are limited—no sane driver would try it. It's not supposed to lift until Saturday night. Maybe."

"Don't you try it either," Val said sharply. "Don't even—I want you safe more than I want you here."

Jamie was not so good at hiding the sniff this time.

"Honey," Val said slowly. "Put down the bowl or pot or whatever. Now just breathe."

Fortunately, Val's voice sounded as thick with unshed tears as hers did. For a minute Jamie could only wipe away tears. Finally, she was able to say, "I miss you so much. It's worse than last year."

"I find myself hugging people," Val admitted. "Not…not in a sleazy, gamey way. Just for the warmth. The contact."

"I know what you mean."

"I'm trying every way I can think of to be away less."

You say that every year, Jamie could have said, but that wasn't the truth that mattered. "I love you, and watching you on TV is no substitute."

"I'm out of your ginger cookies and had the last of the marmalade this morning. I was going to do without for a day to want it all the more."

Jamie had to smile through her misty tears. "I swear you miss the marmalade more than me."

"Honey, after I ravished you for most of Wednesday night, I was going to slather you in the marmalade for Thanksgiving breakfast and consume you whole."

"Oh, that sounds delicious. Now if the fog will lift..." This time she did glance out the window. There was nothing but a white wall out there, pressing its cold misty face against the window screens.

"Not likely, is it?"

Jamie shook her head, unable to answer.

"Then I'll be home on the tenth. It's just two more weeks. I'll be home and maybe we'll just stay home for Christmas. I don't care—the holidays are where you are."

Jamie mopped her eyes on a dish towel. When she could talk again she said, "Mushball. And I love you."

"Two more weeks is forever," Jamie told Lady Dog Puppy. She sat on the mud porch idly petting the glossy coat. They'd gone for a very short walk while the last pies were baking. If Jamie didn't know the breaks in the sidewalk, stairs and potholes outside the Waterview, she might have broken a leg. Val had had to experience one of their blanket fogs to believe her about just barely seeing her hand in front of her face. If the fog didn't lift she wasn't driving anywhere.

And what's more, she had a kitchen full of pies that only a few brave souls would pick up. It was a good thing they were pre-paid, and she'd freeze them, if need be, for when the fog finally did lift, but what a pain. Folks would go without their Thanksgiving desserts. "And I'm going without my lover."

She pouted her way through kitchen cleanup, and a phone call to Liesel telling her to stay home tomorrow. She did get asked to Thanksgiving dinner, an offer she accepted gratefully. She promised to bring pie.

After dinner she tried watching an episode of Val's *A Month of Sundays*. Val in a tool belt was still a sight that made Jamie feel swollen and wonderfully weak. It was hardly helping her frustration with the fog. She browsed through her favorite moments from Val's Iron Chef and Top Chef appearances as a guest judge. Usually, she melted when Val said, "I appreciate the science that went into making this dish. I don't know how to use a laser to cook a shrimp. But I'm not convinced this is cooking. It's sterile, and food should cross the line from art to love." After all, Val was quoting her, and it was a philosophy of cooking they both shared.

No matter, she still missed Val. She gave up on television and dialed up holiday tunes on her iPod. A lovely jazzy number from *A Charlie Brown Christmas* left her smiling. But Karen Carpenter's buttery, low voice failed to comfort. She didn't want to be wishing Val Merry Christmas, darling, from a distance, not ever. Not any of the holidays.

Being apart sucked, and she was sick of it.

Obviously, it was time to bake something.

Anything—but the problem was she had no customers to sell the result to, because of the damned fog. She really needed chocolate too. If she made chocolate goodies she couldn't even feed them to the dog. She'd read lots of places that chocolate and pooches didn't get along.

Peanut butter cookies, maybe. She could feed them to the dog, and top her own with some chocolate ganache. And take the rest to Liesel.

Maybe it didn't smell quite as wonderful as chocolate, but peanut butter, brown sugar and toffee bits filled the kitchen with sweet aromas all the same. For cooking time she settled for something between chewy and crunchy, and frosted a half dozen with ganache. One of those and two plain cookies she took with her out to the porch.

Lady Dog Puppy seemed to really like peanut butter cookies. The tail was definitely wagging the dog, and she chomped so vigorously that bits of cookie fell back out of her mouth. She hunted eagerly for all the escaped crumbs and searched all around Jamie's feet. Finally, she rolled over and gnawed at the toes of Jamie's clogs.

Jamie didn't crunch her own cookie quite as loudly, but the chocolate, peanut butter and toffee worked wonders for her attitude. Hell, her needs were pretty simple too. She was happy cooking for anyone—including a dog.

"So you liked that. You have a discriminating palate." Once she finished her own cookie, she scratched the offered tummy, and let the dog out for a few moments to make one last round about the inn's back yard.

She stood in the doorway and all her loneliness seeped back into her the same way the vapor tried to seep into the house. The fog muffled all noise, and not even the occasional crash of waves beyond the headland bluff was audible. There was a hint of dripping, then Lady Dog Puppy was back, shaking her head. The ear flapping noise made Jamie smile. Silence fell again, without even the distant sound of the highway to break it. She and the dog might have been all that was left on the planet.

With that spine-chilling thought, Jamie didn't feel the least bit guilty when she scooped Lady Dog Puppy up in her arms and carried her upstairs.

"You can't sleep on the bed. You can't shed. You can't bark."

Slurp on the nose.

"I'm serious."

She looked at the off-white carpet, then the dog's paws. A trip to the bathroom sink got Jamie more wet than the dog. She spread a thick towel near the gas-lit fireplace and grinned at the enormous sigh Lady Dog Puppy let out as she settled down. At least she'd made someone happy tonight.

The dog isn't a person, Jamie told herself. She was too tired from baking all day to be awake for long, but her last thought was that she was not replacing Val with a dog. Not in the least. No, she wasn't...

Val had called five times on the drive up from San Francisco, whenever her cell would pick up a signal. Jamie did her rounds of the merchant stores early, with Lady Dog Puppy on a lead. As if to pretend the six days of fog during Thanksgiving week had never happened, the sun blazed yellow and sharp over the deep blue of the white-capped winter Pacific, which rolled for miles to the horizon. There were even a few tourists driving through town, looking for an open eatery and maybe a shop or two. The bookstore was open, and so was one of the artist consignment stores.

The wind off the water was cold, but it blew away every last cobweb in Jamie's brain. She loved Mendocino. She didn't want to leave it. She loved Val too and the past few months had been nearly intolerable.

"I'm going to do it," Jamie said to the dog. "It's time for me to look for a serious partner and spend more of my time in New York with Val. I love running the restaurant. I love being part of the town." She peered into the window of the kitchen gadget and fresh herb store. Nothing seemed amiss. "But every year it's harder to live without her. I don't want to figure out how to live without her, either. If I do that, then..."

She didn't finish the thought. She was certain Lady Dog Puppy knew where that road went. If Jamie figured out how not to miss Val, then why even bother having Val around?

She thought of Val on the highway, knew Val was smiling as she drove. Her body was already warm and melted in anticipation of Val's hands. Tears threatened at the idea of waking up tomorrow and finding Val in their bed, where she belonged.

"The bed in New York isn't hers, it's ours. I belong there too. I'll work on another cookbook. Think of something to keep myself busy." Val could afford to stake her in a restaurant there, but if it didn't pan out—and more than half of all restaurant ventures failed—it would intensify Val's dependence on new projects, guest shoots and more programming. "I know—the Waterview runs like a clock. I love it. I could work on a cookbook here too. If I really wanted to."

The truth was, in New York she was a show biz wife. She enjoyed being social with Val, but it brought out her jealous side when baby dykes checked her out as if they were in some kind of competition. She trusted Val absolutely, and she didn't like herself much in New York. Of course, if she was around more, the baby dykes would find some other star to lust after, and it wouldn't be such an issue.

The headlands were beautiful today—achingly wild as the wind tore across the grass, carrying the scent of the sea. Val was having a beautiful drive. Jamie knew Val wanted to be here. But Val also wanted to be her trademark VV, the home improvement celebrity she was. They'd dreamed often of Val being able to film her second series, *Simplicity*, from the Waterview, or a studio kitchen they created in one of the other buildings that often came up for rent, but the cost was prohibitive.

It was too beautiful an afternoon to be thinking about that. She turned her steps toward home with Lady Dog Puppy happily chasing leaves for as far as the lead would allow.

There was the matter of the dog too. No luck finding a home, and Liesel had refused to keep the dog for a few days while Jamie broke the news and maybe wheedled a dog run for the backyard, and a way for Lady Dog Puppy to get from the mud porch to their living suite without being able to also stray into the kitchen. It could work—if anyone could figure it out, Val could.

Lady Dog Puppy happily made for her water bowl and the rug while Jamie paused to inhale the aroma in the kitchen. Orange and spice mingled with ginger and roasting chicken. The Waterview was closed for the day. Not for a million dollars did Jamie want to be distracted when Val arrived. She had a bowl of chocolate body paint and another of marmalade…and every intention of taking Val up on her offers made over the phone.

The last hour passed quickly, especially with Val calling. It was silly, to be talking to Val as she parked in front of the inn. Jamie burst out the door before Val had even hung up, her heart aching and full, dashing away tears of excitement and happiness. Val caught her with a whoop.

And kissed her.

Kissed her like the first time. Like every time.

She filled her hands with Val's thick, dark hair. The gasped half-sentences they managed to say between kisses didn't matter—they all meant the same thing.

Val pushed Jamie up onto the hood of the car and kissed her one more time. It was an X-rated kind of kiss the singed the bottoms of Jamie's feet.

"We have to go inside."

"Uh huh," Val said. She leaned back and Jamie got her first

good look at her lover.

As always, she thought she was incredibly lucky that this gorgeous woman loved her. Then, with a shock, she realized she was comparing Val's face with Val's publicity photos and the way Val looked on TV. Not with her Val. Her Val was the Val with no make-up, with sleep in her eyes, and hair in wild splendor on the pillows.

She'd forgotten how Val *really* looked.

She blurted out, "I want to come and live with you in New York." And then her chin crumpled and she gulped for air and burst into tears.

"Honey, honey," Val soothed. Her arms were so strong, and so warm.

Jamie thought she would melt with tears and loneliness and the pleasure of Val close to her, finally.

"I mean it, Val. I'm done with living apart."

Val pushed her away just enough to be able to look into Jamie's eyes. Jamie wasn't surprised that Val also had tears in her eyes. "Me too, darling. I have a tenth anniversary gift for you. For us. I wanted to tell you in person."

Val's voice had softened and Jamie's heart leapt to her throat. Val was lit up with a smile that wouldn't quit. Her eyes sparkled, and it had nothing to do with fancy lighting.

"We syndicated to the UK last week. Full rerun package, the last seven years of *A Month of Sundays* and five years of *Simplicity*. And because Sheila got me the best agent in television, I'm going to make nearly as much from the syndication as I did the first time around. I'm home to stay, darling. Happy Anniversary, Merry Christmas, Happy New Year, too."

It took a moment to sink in. Val was going to nearly double her income? Just like that? Syndication…the magic word in television. Slowly, she asked, "We can afford to build a studio for you?"

"Yes—I'm only leaving for location shoots. I'll probably sell the place in New York and use the network's rentals when I have to. I am not spending one more holiday away from you."

Val wrapped her close and didn't seem to mind the tear-soaked shoulder—she never minded.

Jamie finally had the presence of mind to get off the car and take Val inside.

They kissed and snuggled their way into the kitchen where Val took one look at the chocolate body paint and gave Jamie a look that melted her on the spot. "I love the way you plan ahead."

She had just swiped her finger through the luscious, rich mixture when scratching started at the back door.

Jamie decided to ignore it.

Then there was a bark.

Her index finger covered with chocolate, Val gave Jamie an arched eyebrow look. "Is that stray still around?"

"Uh…yes. See, honey, it…"

"Jamie—you can't have a dog in the kitchen."

"She's not in here, see? She's on the porch."

"A dog can't live out there."

"Well…not the way it is now."

Val opened her mouth to add another protest, but then they were both startled by a loud pounding on the front door of the inn. "What in hell is that?"

Jamie walked through the dining room, shaking her head. She got to the door and said loudly, "We're closed. I'm sorry."

She was about to turn away when the middle-aged man on the other side of the glass pressed a paper to the surface.

"Did you put up this sign?"

It was the notice that read "Dog Found" and described Lady Dog Puppy.

"Yes," Jamie said slowly. "I put it up."

"Do you still have the dog?"

"Yes, she's fine."

"Thank God!" He turned his head to call, "She's here, Charlie."

Running footsteps pounded the sidewalk outside and Jamie, feeling more numb than she would have thought possible given Val's wonderful news, found herself opening the door. A little girl with short, wispy pigtails peered up at her.

"Do you have Dora?"

"Well, I have the dog I found. Come on in."

Father and daughter followed her across the empty restaurant and into the kitchen. Val was there, her finger still covered with chocolate. The man blinked at Val like he was trying to figure out how he knew her, but the little girl was following Jamie's every move.

Jamie opened the back door. Lady Dog Puppy moved back, used to Jamie picking her up to smuggle her upstairs.

"Dora!"

Lady Dog Puppy—Dora—let out a yelp and jumped into the little girl's arms.

"Bad dog," the little girl said, between sobs. "You aren't really an explorer. You shouldn't go off on your own."

Tears of joy, Jamie told herself. She had Val back, and for good, and she wouldn't miss the dog. Not much.

She refused the offer of payment from the relieved father. She accepted one last lick across the nose from Dora, though. Dora looked like she belonged with Charlie, and little Charlie was clearly going to trust for the rest of her life that miracles happened.

Dora barked what might have been a thank you as the sedan pulled away, little girl and not quite puppy in the back seat together.

Jamie locked the front door. Val was behind her, arms

around her waist.

"I'm glad for the family, but sad for you, sweetie."

Jamie had thought she might cry, but it passed. Dora was back in her home. It wasn't a sad ending. "I'm okay."

She leaned back in Val's arms. "I don't need a dog if I have you."

"That's gratifying."

Jamie lifted Val's hands from her waist and frowned at the clean fingers. "Where's my chocolate?"

"I thought we'd start over with that. In a bit. I was thinking why not a spiral pet staircase?" Val's voice had an edge of excitement, the way it got when she talked about tearing out walls and hammering stuff. "One from the porch to upstairs and one downstairs to the back yard and a dog run? Electronic collar triggers on the pet doors so we don't get squirrels."

The happiness of Val's announcement was starting to feel real, like something Jamie could keep and count on. Ten years, and they'd finally be together more than they were apart.

Turning in Val's arms, Jamie slipped a hand behind Val's neck. Nuzzling Val's mouth, she said, "We've got a studio to build first. Why don't we talk about all of that tomorrow?"

With a searing look that not one of her viewers had ever seen, Val reached for the bowl of chocolate body paint.

Stepping Stone

Published: 2009
Characters: Selena Ryan, independent film producer
               Gail Welles, actress, waitress
Setting: Hollywood, California

There'd be no twenty-two without all of you.

Action

(18 months)

"Please? Please please *please?*" Gail tugged her ball cap more firmly down on her head. The Santa Ana winds were in full force, raking across the Los Angeles basin like hot blades. "Why are we in a convertible if we're not going to have ice cream cones? It's ninety degrees and it's not even noon."

Selena put the turn signal on, earning a hoot of victory from Gail. "I fail to see what ice cream cones have to do with convertibles."

"It seems like exactly the sort of thing that Kim Novak or Joan Fontaine would do, doesn't it?"

Idling in a red zone, Selena only said, "Get me chocolate."

Gail hopped out of the car, reasonably sure that in hats, glasses and flip flops no one was going to recognize her. It was too hot to be coiffed. She knew her casual appearance would horrify Christopher, but then everything less than couture horrified Christopher. It was so rare that they had a day to just hang out, drive some place, share ice cream.

As she waited for the scoops she watched Lena in the car. She was frowning—probably reviewing her mental To Do list. Lena's latest project was opening production on Monday and last night they had both attended the wrap party for Gail's last movie. It had been a good part—not as much potential as her first one, but as a follow-up it would get solid attention. Catching attention for a major studio-funded project had been good for her credentials.

Their schedule convergence made this weekend rare as platinum, though Gail had to keep herself from demanding too much attention when Lena was trying to focus. Still, a trip to Christopher's and some ice cream seemed a great way to spend a free Saturday afternoon. Tonight they had to get spruced up again, hence the decision to shop.

Chocolate in one hand and already licking her cherry toffee vanilla, she got back to the car in time to hand the cone over just before it dripped on the upholstery.

"It was in your hand," Gail said. "Not my problem."

"It's on *your* seat, so unless you want chocolate on your butt find a napkin. And technically this is your car, remember?"

"Oh yeah." Gail was still not used to the idea that she could own a BMW convertible, but her ancient Corolla had died in glorious fashion on the 110 earlier in the summer. She dabbed at the spot with some water from the ubiquitous bottle in the cup holder. "All better."

"So where do I turn for Christopher's?"

"Next left. I can't believe you've never been there. Kim sent me there right off."

"Kim knows my tastes well. Vintage stuff looks awesome on you, darling, but I'm a less flashy type."

"What are we giving her for a wedding gift?"

That topic occupied the two of them the rest of the drive. Gail had been glad to see Lena's assistant walking on air since meeting Mr. Right. She truly hoped it lasted. And ice cream for lunch was dandy.

"This is it?" Selena pulled into a parking space across the street from Christopher's pink-framed door. "All that fabulous clothing is in there?"

"I know it looks unlikely—you'll understand. C'mon slowpoke!"

Selena watched her wife skip across the street. In board shorts, A-shirt, flip flops and a Dodger hat Gail looked like a fifteen-year old boy. There were a million things she ought to be doing right now and none of them was more important than watching Gail lick an ice cream cone.

She followed at a more sedate pace—she hadn't skipped in years and maybe that was a shame and maybe she was saving her strength for the surprise she had planned for later, when they were home, alone, and could sleep in as late as they wanted. A romantic evening alone together was badly needed.

She smiled to herself and entered the store in time to hear a tenor-ranged male voice say, "What on *earth* are you wearing?"

"No one's going to recognize me, Christopher. I'm just not famous enough."

"You'd be more famous if they'd given you that Oscar you deserved. Well, you're not getting fat. Good." The angular, elderly man placed a bookmark in his book, closed it and set it at the end of his tidy counter. It looked like a memoir of Quentin Crisp.

"What's that got to do with anything?" Gail took a

provocatively big bite out of her cone. "Weight standards in Hollywood are sexist."

"Of course they are. You didn't know this when you decided to come here?" His arched eyebrow glance shifted from Gail to Selena. He regarded her owlishly through thick glasses for a moment, then said, "Ms. Ryan, I presume?"

"I've heard a lot about you, and decided to tag along," she said, looking around her. The walls were neatly draped with old movie posters, most sealed in plexiglass frames. The clothing racks were spaced out with a number of antique standing mirrors placed between them.

"Welcome to my humble store, then. It's good to see one of you doesn't completely throw fashion to the wind just because it's a bit hot out."

Selena wasn't sure if she should thank him for the compliment. Bermuda shorts, sandals, a thin cotton polo shirt... She was glad to know she passed muster but she hadn't given it much thought.

"Gail, my dear, I've several outfits for you to consider. Come right this way."

A personal shopper always on the lookout for just the right thing was a nice plus in life, Selena decided. Gail was tall and gangly, and though she'd grown her hair a little bit longer, and Selena didn't know how anyone could mistake her full, beautiful lips and delicate curved brow for a guy's, it still happened. It was, as Gail said, the lack of boobs—not that Selena had any complaint about that. What Gail had was very responsive and...not something she should be thinking about in a clothing store, she told herself. Later.

"These are legitimate Chanel," he announced, unzipping a wide garment bag. The turquoise is you, the rose will work, but I have my doubts about the chartreuse—oh dear God, no. No, let's put that one right away." He shuddered as he transferred the offending garment to a different rack.

If Christopher hadn't been at least seventy, Selena would have found his Big Queen act cloying, but she had a feeling he was an original, and at his age he could do as he liked. "I like that rose color. She has this fetching little hat—"

"The Rosalind Russell hat, yes it's perfect. You have an excellent eye, Ms. Ryan."

"Call me Selena, please."

"Harry Cohn never let me call him anything but Mr. Cohn."

"Harry Cohn never let *anybody* call him anything but Mr. Cohn—except perhaps Rita Hayworth."

"That sweet lady could call anyone anything and they'd love her for it. I was honored to cut cloth for her in *Salome*."

Selena smiled. "The costumes were gorgeous."

"They were. Jean Louis should have been nominated for his designs. They were exquisite." His gaze turned back to Gail, who was frowning at the teal jacket and skirt with big black buttons and yellow braid. "Not that you could wear any of them. But you *can* wear that. Darling, you'll intimidate the super models, I mean, they are required to make that outfit look smashing, but you do it just because you can."

"Would it look okay for an outdoor award kind of thing?"

"What kind of *thing* exactly?"

"Tonight my friend Hyde is getting a star on the Walk of Fame."

Christopher didn't squeak, but Selena thought that was just because the sound he made was out of her range of hearing. Elsewhere in the neighborhood it was possible that dogs had begun barking. "That man makes me perspire. He's Glenn Ford and Randolph Scott all rolled up together."

"Well, he's a sweetheart too, and I also need something to wear to his wedding, which is going to be a quiet affair."

"How does he think he'll manage that?"

"Private island out of range of helicopters from anywhere

else." Selena happily spread the cover story. The wedding was actually taking place a week earlier than their leaked information would let on, and it was limited to only those people Hyde and his bride called family. Gail was family to him, a little sister that he confided secrets to. He sometimes sought Selena's advice on a role, and she was pleased that she had indeed earned his respect. There was a script on her desk right now that, with rewrites, might work for him.

"I might have something for that—a copy of the cocktail dress Grace Kelly wore in *To Catch a Thief*, or it might have been *Rear Window*. Simple, would fit tropical weather."

"I'm no Grace Kelly," Gail said.

"Oh course not, but she didn't possess a particularly fulsome figure. She was shorter than you by four inches or so, but the dress I'm thinking of was cut to a demure length. Still, we can give it a try as the date draws closer. I have a number of other party dresses that won't shame me."

Obviously, Christopher took his role as Gail's dresser seriously. It was very nice to see her still struggling-to-be-noticed-and-not-always-as-The-Lesbian wife given star treatment.

"These two items came in last month from an estate sale. This one you are too young for, but it will likely work in future years—the cut is too good a fit for you to pass up." He set aside a tweed suit and held up instead a sleeveless princess-cut dress in black brocade, embellished with a great many black sequins. It made Selena mindful of Audrey Hepburn. Gail had these sexy little boots that would be really fetching with it too.

The last suit she thought a bit ho hum in beige but no one had asked her opinion yet. Her interest in fashion had pretty much been exhausted by the time Gail and Christopher had discussed the trim and hem. Ecru, ivory, mushroom— whatever. It went the way of the chartreuse suit, leaving Gail with the two Chanels, the tweed and the dress.

"You try these on, then." He imperiously gestured toward

the back of the store. "You know where."

Selena tagged along. She saw no reason to miss Gail removing her clothes. She liked the dressing room too. There was a Victorian love seat for her to lounge in while Gail tried on clothes. The whole dressing room was done in deep red brocade, including the walls, making it much like a lady's boudoir.

The tweed jacket and skirt were first and they fit like glove. He was right, the outfit made Gail look older—it was very Joan Fontaine traveling-on-the-continent, and it screamed class and elegance. "Wear that to an audition when you need to age up," she suggested. "You don't look like a boy in the least in it."

"I never do in vintage clothes." Gail began unbuttoning the jacket again. "Christopher says I was born fifty years too late and if I got a boob job I'd have designers clamoring to fit me."

"Only get one if you want one."

"I don't." Gail glanced down at her chest. Her thin, skin-toned sport bra was more than adequate to the job of maintaining Gail's modesty. "They're not much but they're mine."

"And I appreciate that you let me visit." She didn't say another word but was gratified to see Gail flush.

"Stop that—later. Lots of time for that later."

"If you say so."

The Chanel suits were next. Both were pronounced suitable and taken off again, leaving the Audrey Hepburn style dress. If anything it could be too narrow in the hip, Selena thought, which was hard to believe.

"Who would that have originally been made for?" She knew she didn't have a hope of ever being that small.

Christopher's voice floated over the enclosure wall. "If you mean the sheath, I was told it was designed for Twiggy, *the*

Twiggy, but she never wore it. Darlings, I simply must run down the street to my bank. They close in just a bit—Saturday hours. Is it all right if I lock you in? I won't be ten minutes."

"No worries," Gail called.

"I'll put a note on the door before I lock it. If someone rings, just ignore it."

The little bell at the entrance chimed and then the shop was silent.

"Zip?" Gail turned her back and Selena rose to ease the zipper up Gail's spine. She added a little nip at the nape of Gail's neck, just because.

"Later. What do you think?" Gail turned from the mirror. "It's very…elegant lady."

"It's very you," Selena said. Her eyes traced the outline of Gail's slender hips. "It fits beautifully."

"Except here." Gail pointed to one arm pit. "It's a little binding."

"Take off the sport bra—I think that's the issue. It looks like it's already lined so you wouldn't have to wear anything." She unzipped the dress again and Gail slid it off her shoulders.

Selena lifted off Gail's Dodger cap just before Gail pulled the bra over her head. She gave Gail's hair a quick ruffle, then—being no fool—she swept her hands around to cup Gail's breasts.

Gail sucked in her breath. "We'll be here all day if you do that."

"I wouldn't mind." She loved the way Gail's shoulder blades tightened. A telltale red flush was creeping along her shoulders.

"The dress," Gail said weakly.

"Oh yes, the dress." She tried to assume a business-like air as she zipped it up.

Gail looked at herself in the mirror, then met Selena's gaze. "Given that my nipples are like rocks right now and they don't show I think you're right. I can go without a bra. It's a perfect fit."

"Perfect," Selena echoed. "That is a killer little black dress."

She had the zipper halfway down Gail's back when she came to her senses. They were alone. They had at least eight minutes left. She of all people knew the value of eight minutes. There was no reason to move this moment to later in their day. Gail was still flushed and her own heart was abruptly pounding.

The zipper now down to the base of Gail's spine, she pushed the dress off Gail's shoulders. Not giving her any time to react, she firmly pressed her face first into the wall next to the mirror and let the dress fall around her ankles.

"Lena, we—oh…"

Her fingernails on just the tips of Gail's nipples silenced the protest. "We have just enough time, I think. I didn't get where I am not knowing when to say 'action.'"

Gail started to laugh but was silenced again by Selena yanking down her panties. For a minute it was simply sublime to press her entire body against Gail's quivering warmth, her lips brushing over the heat of Gail's neck.

"What if—"

"We'll stop. But I want to finish at least this." She slipped her hand between them. "Spread your legs for me, darling. Please… Oh yes."

Gail shuddered and her back curved deliciously in invitation. Selena's fingers were swimming as she cupped all of Gail's wonderful wetness in her hand.

"No time for teasing, darling, though I know how much you like that." Selena's head was spinning at the measure of Gail's surrender—it always affected her that way. Her voice was almost a stranger's, coming from a part of her that only Gail had ever heard. "I'm going to just have you, right now."

Gail braced both hands on the wall with a long, guttural moan. "Yes, yes Lena."

Part of her was listening for the bell, but most of her was reveling in the way she slipped inside Gail with a long, firm push. She withdrew, felt as well as heard Gail groan, then she was in again, harder. And harder.

Panting, Gail was pushing back, the lean lines of her hips rippling as Selena ground against her. It felt fantastic to touch her, to be inside, to feel muscles gripping at her fingers in response to her touch. She kissed Gail's neck and tasted salt and suddenly their bodies were both slick with sweat from the fire burning between them.

Gail let out a long moan and her knees buckled. Selena caught her, pushed in one last time and savored every quiver against her fingertips, and every spasm of nerves as she slowly withdrew and cupped her again. She lightly caressed every fold and wet place, drawing a gasp and then a slow, satisfied sigh from Gail as they both carefully sank to the floor.

"That was…fun."

Gail cleared her throat and twisted around to give Selena an incredulous look. "Fun? Fun is for board games. That was—what if we'd gotten caught? What ever would we say to Kim and the rest of the staff if we'd ended up somebody's daily dish?"

"I thought there was a low chance of getting caught, and a high chance of really, really enjoying ourselves." She helped Gail to her feet and found herself pulled into a fervent embrace.

"I know there's not enough time, but tonight I am going to…" The kiss that followed was a promise and Selena was more than ready to see what they could manage in the possible two minutes they had left, but Gail's saner head prevailed.

And that was a good thing because Christopher returned in nine minutes, not ten. Gail was back in her clothes and

Selena had visited the rest room. Now that it was over, she dearly hoped they'd left no trace. Nevertheless, she was always going to agree to go shopping in the future.

The garments all wrapped and tied, Gail signed the bill and gave Christopher a parting hug.

"Have fun at the ceremony tonight. Do give that beast of a man a hug from me."

"I will," Gail said.

"When I was out I thought the winds were finally dying down. Enjoy the rest of your lazy day," he added. "It already looks like it's doing you both good."

They were in the car before they burst into mutual, guilty laughter.

With Frosting You Get Sprinkles

Hello readers. Thank you.

I could stop there. It's really the most important thing I have to say.

But those of you who have followed my history of blogging, listserv activity and Facebook postings know I'm unlikely to stop there, not when I've a blank page that needs filling.

The first *Frosting on the Cake* was published in 2001. At that time *blogging, listserv* and *Facebook* were not words in my lexicon. *Friend* was not a verb and complete sentences were a laudable goal. What's the world coming to? idk wtf cu bff

Though the craft of writing hasn't changed much, the process of putting a book out into the world has. Nevertheless, every book represents a labor of love by a team of women. I'm very glad that remains the same.

One comment about this section of the book—I've been graced by my publishers with remarkable editors, especially the mentorship of Katherine V. Forrest. There are writers who believe that they don't need an editor, but this writer does as this unedited, from the heart but not Chicago Manual section will prove. All my bad habits are up for your scrutiny. Just me here. What's a dangling participle again?

Something else hasn't changed about my creative process and that's the way characters come alive for me. When I began working on this collection of stories, I made up a list of all the novels I'd written since the last volume. The last novel I'd published at that time was *Unforgettable*. In that first *Frosting* volume, my notes about each book stopped there. So…let's pick up where we left off.

Substitute for Love

I was watching the Cheney-Lieberman vice presidential debate in 2000. In response to a question about marriage equality, Cheney managed to sound almost…liberal. Yet I knew where he stood on the issue. He was running for office so he was against it. (When he got out of office suddenly he wasn't. Thanks, Dick.) So I wondered, as I watched Dick talk, what it would feel like to be his daughter and listen to him sound like he thought you deserved equal civil rights and knowing he would sacrifice you in a heartbeat on the altar of his ambition. That was the birth of Reyna Putnam and her grim Darth Vader father. In "Reconciliation" she still lives with the double-edged gift—he is silent, but his reach is long.

As for Holly Markham, the inspiration was not nearly so topical. I wanted a character who had a gift, but one that hadn't been nurtured. I needed an exceptional woman who just didn't know it yet. I knew nothing about high-end mathematics, but I knew that one of Barbie's pull-on-the-string sayings was "Math is hard!" So why not a mathematician whose family devalued her skills because men don't go ballistic for girls who dig statistics. Last, and meant to be least, was the character of Clay, Holly's boyfriend, who busily squelched every impulse she had, disguising his overbearing selfishness as new age sensitivity. Let's just say that when I gritted my teeth and wrote the paper that professor wanted to read about his politics being superior and better thought out than anyone else's that I knew he'd show up in a book some day.

Maybe Next Time

A word to the wise for other writers who work from inside a character's head. If you create a character who has only one way to communicate with the world, don't take that away until after you have what you need. Otherwise, you're going to be staring at a lot of blank pages for a long time. Sabrina Starling remains a difficult and uncooperative character to this day—you'll have noticed there is no short story inspired by this novel for you to read. I checked in with Sabrina, my one-time suicidal violinist, and this is all I got back: *If the earth doesn't move, then there's no earthquake.*

That's it. She refused to say another word. So I guess that all is well and nothing has happened in her life that she feels is worth mentioning. She does live in one of the most beautiful parts of the world, Hawaii's Kona coast. The sun goes up, the sun goes down and if there are Christmas lights it might be December. Otherwise, hang loose.

Thank goodness not all characters are like Bree. I put her through a wringer and she repaid me in full measure. But our intense synergy resulted in my first Lambda Literary Award, which was also the first award of any kind I'd ever won for my writing. It was also my first romance written for Bella Books—a promising start to what has become a beautiful relationship.

One Degree of Separation

It won't be a newsflash to anyone if I say that my first crush on a real live woman was on a librarian. I was old enough to be checking out my own books. A man had come to the library to say that he was not going to pay for a book that he hadn't returned. It was a vulgar book, full of profanity, and he'd thrown it away. (The book? *Gravity's Rainbow* by Thomas Pynchon.) The librarian explained that a library was a public trust. She said a lot more and truly, all I remember is thinking that she could be Barbara Gordon because she was wonderful and heroic and marvelous. She was wearing a sweater set, knit skirt, sensible shoes and glasses and she had pencils stuck through her tight bun. The cape must have been invisible, but I could still see it.

Flash forward a couple of decades and Marian the librarian from Iowa City was born. Though I gave her many human traits—hormones from hell, migraines and a sarcastic wit that got her into trouble—she was still a superhero to me. I was so fond of Marian that I conjured up Liddy, just for her, added a case of instant attraction and a reservoir of untapped, mutual sexual energy. For Marian, her identity as a butch was one she chose and embraced, even if for some she just wasn't "mannish" enough. For Liddy, her dislike of being thought femme was rooted in the stereotype that she was supposed to be helpless. Swear to freakin' god, Liddy was anything but. They were the first explicitly butch/femme couple I'd written since *Touchwood*, and it won't be the last time I explore labels within the lesbian community. Labels can be fun and useful, they can honor—or they can hurt. They can illuminate our identity—or limit it.

All the Wrong Places

At the same time I was writing these last few books I was also writing erotica. During a vacation to a Club Med resort,

I had a lot of fun imagining different hijinx behind the scenes and in one of those quick sketches of story ideas I found the character of my physical fitness instructor, Brandy Monsoon. Young, brash, sexually open, frequent visitor to the Good Vibrations Web store and willing to experiment, she found sex easy. Love, well, not so much. When easygoing encounters with her friend-with-benefits co-worker Tess turned emotionally terrifying she hadn't a clue what was happening to her. Even now, completely opposite from my relationship with Sabrina in *Maybe Next Time*, I ask Brandy what's up and she has a story to tell, usually about how things that seem simple, like saying "Let's be exclusive" to the woman you're madly in love with, really aren't simple at all. Both of the stories in this collection were originally published in erotica anthologies; they've both been altered and amplified because Brandy always has just a little bit more to say.

Sugar

When I watch a cooking show I feel as if I could pluck any ingredient out of the ground, slap it around with some EVOO and I am an Iron Chef. Right.

My passion for food and cooking shows up in many of my novels—I can safely say that my family wishes I had a fraction of the skill of my heroines. Enter Sugar Sorenson, who works with the one thing I have the sense not to try: fondant. Sweet Sugar was my ace of cakes before there was an Ace of Cakes. She was also my homage to the self-employed entrepreneur. Too busy to fall in love, her life refuses to stop for even a minute to let her catch her breath. She doesn't have time to meet women—so I arranged for women to meet her. A purely fun read, *Sugar* marked my first of five Golden Crown Literary Awards.

Just Like That

Where would we be without Jane Austen? She wrote the first "literary" romance and was soundly trashed by (male) critics, writers and readers of her era for that hysterical nonsense about how women think and feel. Her heroines were bright with intelligence, modest in beauty and the embodiment—in one form or another—of the limitations of a gentlewoman's social standing and financial realities. In my favorite Austen work, *Pride and Prejudice*, Elizabeth Bennet proudly spurns the arrogant Mr. Darcy and his ten thousand pounds a year even though she is on the brink of abject poverty. When he returns, fully appreciating the beautiful expression of her dark eyes, they have both changed and the course of true love is finally smoothed.

I had written about seventy-five percent of *Just Like That* before I realized I was basically retelling *Pride and Prejudice*, but in a very lesbian way. Syrah and Toni both allowed prejudice and pride to rule their emotions. I committed fully to the concept by paraphrasing one of the most famous first lines in all of literature: "It is a truth universally acknowledged, that a single man in possession of a good fortune, must be in want of a wife."

18th & Castro

A sharp-eyed reader will have already realized there is no short story based on *18th & Castro* here. The explanation is simple: it's a collection of erotic short stories and it was impossible to decide if any of those 35-40 characters had another story to tell. I do count it as my eighteenth "novel" however, because the stories were tied together with two common threads, and when read together they created a mosaic of sexual expression, primarily for couples.

I've been asked many times why I choose to write erotica. For some readers, it's the same thing as smut—and definitely not their cup of tea. For me, when I looked around at the erotica being produced, I noticed a distinct lack of storytelling around long-term couples. *18th & Castro* gave me a chance to explore how couples relate through sex. I also wanted to decriminalize sex for lesbians. Nice girls do, after all. They do all sorts of things, and they're still nice girls.

Finders Keepers

If we all loved our bodies the way they were we wouldn't spend a minute trying to change them. But I don't know a woman who isn't trying to change something about herself. Having struggled all my life with image and weight, creating Marissa Chabot was easy. It was also easy to give her a moment of epiphany: change or die. As she struggled on her journey through the book to find fitness and better health, a lot of my own research into weight control and healthy fitness was put to good use. Anyone who has read my online document about the background research of the novel will recognize this sentiment: exercise sucks, mostly because it works and makes me feel better. A pox on it!

While it was relatively easy to create an overweight character who desperately wanted to change, it felt unbalanced to limit the story to one kind of body image issue. Everywhere we look there are beautiful, thin women. I don't think most are happy with their bodies either. And, regardless of her body image, if a woman hates a part of herself, how does she have the capacity to completely love someone else? These are not easy issues, and I tried my best not to create easy answers. It's a struggle, a journey, but in the case of Marissa and Linda, it became a journey that was easier together.

Finders Keepers is not the first novel where I dealt with child abuse and its lingering effect on a grown woman. There were readers, however, who "didn't buy it." One in particular felt strongly that the kind of abuse I detailed couldn't have been hidden from other family members, teachers or doctors. Sadly, it often is. My fictional story was unfortunately inspired by a very real one.

I think the most puzzling—and saddest—reaction was the protest that abuse didn't happen in homes like that, meaning the homes of wealthy people. Abuse knows no socioeconomic boundaries. It is everywhere, including partner abuse in our own community, which was a theme in *One Degree of Separation*. So as part of my writing about real life women I will continue to weave this other reality into stories, but I hope in ways that affirm and uplift as well as empower us to help ourselves or use our eyes to see women and children in bad situations.

The Kiss that Counted

What if a thief fell in love with an elf? Thieves dwell in the dark, elves in the light, so where would they meet? That's the basic genesis of *The Kiss that Counted*. CJ believes that her very DNA is saturated with malice, greed and cruelty. Her childhood and adolescence taught her how to be a thief and a liar. Though she is trying to atone, she believes that she could fall back into that life at any moment, and she has no conviction that she can offer another woman anything of value, not even a real name.

As a comfort to a very lonely and odd-girl-out child, Karita's grandmother raised her believing that she had magic in her blood. Karita knows it's not true, but she wishes it were. Her world is golden, people are good and when bad things happen, all good need do is stand its ground. She finds CJ's darkness inexplicable, and CJ finds Karita's innocence baffling. The vast gulf between their way of looking at the world and understanding of what they can contribute to it was a grand story to write, and I loved the many layers of character development I was able to explore.

The Kiss that Counted won the second of my three Lambda

Literary Awards.

Warming Trend

What began as a writing exercise blossomed into one of my favorite romps across the page. The exercise was explaining why an expert in glaciers would live in Key West, Florida (nearest glacier at least 2,000 miles away). A love affair gone wrong seemed a good answer to me, but my heroine wasn't the type to fall in love with the wrong woman. Why would she run from the right woman then? Ah, enter the Femme Fatale with a Messiah Complex. Poor, poor Ani and Eve.

One of the joys of writing character-driven fiction is when an incidental character blossoms into much more. Ani's loyal new best friend forever, Lisa, started as a quick fling, but Lisa promptly informed me that she didn't go where she wasn't wanted, it was plain Ani was still hung up on Eve and besides, something was rotten in the state of Alaska. Who got Ani on a plane for home? Did Ani or Eve figure out exactly what had happened on that fateful glacier expedition and why Ani took the blame? No, of course not. Lisa had to do it all by herself, well, mostly. It was great fun to revisit Lisa when writing "Good Morning," once again through Ani's long-suffering point-of-view.

The novel also features a great dog. Tonk has no prototype in real life, though. I have teenagers to feed so a Newfoundland is right out.

Stepping Stone

Some novels are about characters who are focused on a singular goal in life, and along the way their paths cross but the two paths refuse to become one. *Wild Things* comes to mind—Faith and Sydney are inseparable, but neither deviates from the path she's on. Instead, they shape the world so their paths overlap. Like Brandy Monsoon, Faith is another character who always has a story to tell, and the stress on their separate careers is the subject of "Losing Faith."

Stepping Stone is another example, set in the most relationship-perilous landscape of all: Hollywood. The joy of writing this story came from my love of film and the strong women in it, and the most satisfying aspect was skewering the nasty blogosphere that reaches lows of "journalism" (and atrocious grammar) that would have made Louella Parsons and Hedda Hopper blanche. With a side industry invested in making a buck by exposing every private moment in a business where your business is already everybody else's business, how can two women hope to have a moment to themselves, and how do they develop the trust it takes to work on a future? The impediments are many, the chance of success small and yet, as so many of us believe, love will find a way.

The story is full of little nods to favorite films and strong women. As always, Barbara Stanwyck comes to mind, as she does whenever I think of *Making Up for Lost Time* and Val in her famous tool belt. You'll have to consult the first *Frosting* volume for that story.

Above Temptation

Not being one of those writers with a lot of work in a drawer waiting to be mined, I finally reached into the small stack and pulled out *Above Temptation*. Originally written years ago in the hopes of publication for a straight audience, the story still worked. All the research behind it would have to be redone, and massive changes in the world of banking, computers and even travel had taken place, forcing both big and small changes throughout the manuscript. By the time I was done there was little of the original left—except for Kip Barrett. Strong, principled and driven, Kip was still waiting for a challenge, so I gave her a crime to investigate from an unexpected client.

Contrary to any beliefs otherwise, lesbian romances aren't straight romances with one of the characters' gender changed. In the early days of my writing career, there were gay and straight critics who described our romances in those terms. (It always made me suspicious of their powers of observation.) Regardless, Tamara Sterling bears little resemblance to the hero I first paired Kip with. Exhausted and heartsick, her reaction to discovering an embezzler among her own staff moves her completely out of her comfort zone. Neither woman is looking for a relationship but both of them know that they are in deep trouble from almost the moment they meet.

Like *Warming Trend, Car Pool* and *The Kiss that Counted*, I liked the added element of a puzzle that the two women work together to solve. I have no desire to write a mystery but it's certainly fun to tie a Gordian knot and figure out how the characters will find and use their sword to set themselves free.

Frosting on the Cake 2: Second Helpings

This project began almost the moment the first *Frosting on the Cake* was sent to typeset. I heard Louisa's voice from *Touchwood* and wrote "The Curve of Her" and otherwise filled in creative down time with sketches for other short stories. I partnered with other writers for anthologies and sometimes drew on previous characters, hence the assortment of stories based on a cruise and in Las Vegas. Sometimes events in real life would make me wonder how a character would react. I can't read about censorship of LGBT titles in public libraries without thinking of Marian my librarian and her horror at the very idea. A chance song on the radio reminds me of books and inspires new ones. It's not a bad life, being a walking sponge. Sooner or later it all gets squeezed out into a story of some kind, and thank goodness, else I would explode.

Where I remain most fortunate is that readers—that's

you—are willing to check out the latest effort. You are there to offer praise and insight or to share a laugh. I'm happy to have met so many of you in person and hope to keep that up. Most of all, your support of lesbian writers keeps this wonderful wheel of creativity, affirmation and entertainment turning.

I only have one regret as a writer: I didn't keep a list of all the character names I'd used in a project. I recommend this to all first-time novelists. Make a list or you'll end up renaming characters halfway through a book—trust me, you won't find them all.

As I said at the beginning of this section, while much has changed in the last decade, some things have not. I ended the first volume with these sentiments, and they are still true: *I am a lucky woman, and I have all of you to thank.*

Publications from
Bella Books, Inc.
Women. Books. Even Better Together.

P.O. Box 10543
Tallahassee, FL 32302
Phone: 800-729-4992
www.bellabooks.com

THE GRASS WIDOW by Nanci Little. Aidan Blackstone is nineteen, unmarried and pregnant, and has no reason to think that the year 1876 won't be her last. Joss Bodett has lost her family but desperately clings to their land. A richly told story of frontier survival that picks up with the generation of women where Patience and Sarah left off.
978-1-59493-189-5 $12.95

SMOKEY O by Celia Cohen. Insult "Mac" MacDonnell and insult the entire Delaware Blue Diamond team. Smokey O'Neill has just insulted Mac, and then finds she's been traded to Delaware. The games are not limited to the baseball field!
978-1-59493-198-7 $12.95

WICKED GAMES by Ellen Hart. Never have mysteries and secrets been closer to home in this eighth installment of this award-winning lesbian mystery series. Jane Lawless's neighbors bring puzzles and peril—and that's just the beginning.
978-1-59493-185-7 $14.95

NOT EVERY RIVER by Robbi McCoy. It's the hottest city in the U.S., and it's not just the weather that's heating up. For Kim and Randi are forced to question everything they thought they knew about themselves before they can risk their fiery hearts on the biggest gamble of all.
978-1-59493-182-6 $14.95

HOUSE OF CARDS by Nat Burns. Cards are played, but the game is gossip. Kaylen Strauder has never wanted it to be about her. But the time is fast-approaching when she must decide which she needs more: her community or Eda Byrne.
978-1-59493-203-8 $14.95

RETURN TO ISIS by Jean Stewart. The award-winning Isis sci-fi series features Jean Stewart's vision of a committed colony of women dedicated to preserving their way of life, even after the apocalypse. Mysteries have been forgotten, but survival depends on remembering. Book one in series. 978-1-59493-193-2 $12.95

1ST IMPRESSIONS by Kate Calloway. Rookie PI Cassidy James has her first case. Her investigation into the murder of Erica Trinidad's uncle isn't welcomed by the local sheriff, especially since the delicious, seductive Erica is their prime suspect. First in series. Author's augmented and expanded edition.
978-1-59493-192-5 $12.95

BEACON OF LOVE by Ann Roberts. Twenty-five years after their families put an end to a relationship that hadn't even begun, Stephanie returns to Oregon to find many things have changed...except her feelings for Paula. 978-1-59493-180-2 $14.95

ABOVE TEMPTATION by Karin Kallmaker. It's supposed to be like any other case, except this time they're chasing one of their own. As fraud investigators Tamara Sterling and Kip Barrett try to catch a thief, they realize they can have anything they want—except each other.
978-1-59493-179-6 $14.95

AN EMERGENCE OF GREEN by Katherine V. Forrest. Carolyn had no idea her new neighbor jumped the fence to enjoy her swimming pool. The discovery leads to choices she never anticipated in an intense, sensual story of discovery and risk, consequences and triumph. Originally released in 1986.
978-1-59493-217-5 $14.95

CRAZY FOR LOVING by Jaye Maiman. Officially hanging out her shingle as a private investigator, Robin Miller is getting her life on track. Just as Robin discovers it's hard to follow a dead man, she walks in. KT Bellflower, sultry and devastating... Lammy winner and second in series.
978-1-59493-195-6 $14.95

LOVE WAITS by Gerri Hill. The All-American girl and the love she left behind—it's been twenty years since Ashleigh and Gina parted, and now they're back to the place where nothing was simple and love didn't wait.
978-1-59493-186-4 $14.95

HANNAH FREE: THE BOOK by Claudia Allen. Based on the film festival hit movie starring Sharon Gless. Hannah's story is funny, scathing and witty as she navigates life with aplomb—but always comes home to Rachel. 32 pages of color photographs plus bonus behind-the-scenes movie information.
978-1-59493-172-7 $19.95

END OF THE ROPE by Jackie Calhoun. Meg Klein has two enduring loves—horses and Nicky Hennessey. Nicky is there for her when she most needs help, but then an attractive vet throws Meg's carefully balanced world out of kilter.
978-1-59493-176-5 $14.95

THE LONG TRAIL by Penny Hayes. When schoolteacher Blanche Bartholomew and dance hall girl Teresa Stark meet their feelings are powerful—and completely forbidden—in Starcross Texas. In search of a safe future, they flee, daring to take a covered wagon across the forbidding prairie.
978-1-59493-196-3 $12.95

UP UP AND AWAY by Catherine Ennis. Sarah and Margaret have a video. The mob wants it. Flying for their lives, two women discover more than secrets.
978-1-59493-215-1 $12.95

CITY OF STRANGERS by Diana Rivers. A captive in a gilded cage, young Solene plots her escape, but the rulers of Hernorium have other plans for Solene—and her people. Breathless lesbian fantasy story also perfect for teen readers.
978-1-59493-183-3 $14.95

ROBBER'S WINE by Ellen Hart. Belle Dumont is the first dead of summer. Jane Lawless, Belle's old friend, suspects coldhearted murder. Lammy-winning seventh novel in critically acclaimed mystery series.
978-1-59493-184-0 $14.95

APPARITION ALLEY by Katherine V. Forrest. Kate Delafield has solved hundreds of cases, but the one that baffles her most is her own shooting. Book six in series.
978-1-883523-65-7 $14.95

STERLING ROAD BLUES by Ruth Perkinson. It was a simple declaration of love. But the entire state of Virginia wants to weigh in, leaving teachers Carrie Tomlinson and Audra Malone caught in the crossfire—and with love troubles of their own.
978-1-59493-187-1 $14.95

LILY OF THE TOWER by Elizabeth Hart. Agnes Headey, taking refuge from a storm at the Netherfield estate, stumbles into dark family secrets and something more… Meticulously researched historical romance.
978-1-59493-177-2 $14.95

LETTING GO by Ann O'Leary. Kelly has decided that luscious, successful Laura should be hers. For now. Laura might even be agreeable. But where does that leave Kate?
978-1-59493-194-9 $12.95

MURDER TAKES TO THE HILLS by Jessica Thomas. Renovations, shady business deals, a stalker—and it's not even tourist season yet for PI Alex Peres and her best four-legged pal Fargo. Sixth in this Provincetown-based series.
978-1-59493-178-9 $14.95

SOLSTICE by Kate Christie. It's Emily Mackenzie's last college summer and meeting her soccer idol Sam Delaney seems like a dream come true. But Sam's passion seems reserved for the field of play…
978-1-59493-175-8 $14.95

FORTY LOVE by Diana Simmonds. Lush, romantic story of love and tennis with two women playing to win the ultimate prize. Revised and updated author's edition.
978-1-59493-190-1 $14.95

I LEFT MY HEART by Jaye Maiman. The only woman she ever loved is dead, and sleuth Robin Miller goes looking for answers. First book in Lammy-winning series.
978-1-59493-188-8 $14.95

TWO WEEKS IN AUGUST by Nat Burns. Her return to Chincoteague Island is a delight to Nina Christie until she gets her dose of Hazy Duncan's renown ill-humor. She's not going to let it bother her, though…
978-1-59493-173-4 $14.95